CORNIX SINISTRA

CORNIX SINISTRA

STEVEN C. DAVIS

Published by Tenebrous Texts

www.tenebrousarchives.weebly.com

First published in Great Britain in 2010
by Tenebrous Texts

Cornix Sinistra (2020 edition)
Book 1 of 'The Bookshop between the Worlds'.

© Steven C. Davis 2010 – 2020
Cover art © Carolin Southern 2010 – 2020
Author photo by LM Cooke.

A CIP catalogue record for this book is available through the British Library.

Typeset by Tenebrous Texts

www.tenebrousarchives.weebly.com

Contents

Dedication and Thanks

Thank you to Victoria Yogman, for supplying countless ideas, for providing critical feedback at important stages and endless cups of tea.
Thanks to Paul Langridge, Guy Robinson and Anna Kutner for praise and questions in equal measure.

A big thank you to Dave Wagstaffe for allowing me use of Bridge. Bridge was our co-creation, written for a TV drama series, circa 2000. Although it wasn't accepted, the character was too interesting to not be used.

Thanks to Carolin for the cover art and a link back to a half-forgotten past.

Gratitude must be expressed to the Open University for their advanced creative writing course, which got me into short stories after years of working on novels.

To Dave Wagstaffe, yet again, for re-igniting the flame.
And to the one for whom the flame burns.

And finally. Thank you to Brian Stableford for a night class in writing Science Fiction all those years ago. Lessons have been taken to heart. I started as close to the end as I could.

And to Xavier and Tenebrous Texts, without whom ...

Jacaranda's Journey

The book was old and large. It was top and tailed with heavy plates, but there was no lock on it as she might have expected. It was strange to the touch, the binding: sometimes like leather, sometimes like silk. The parchment inside was old; authentic without needing to check. It smelled of dust and insects: could well have been mouldering in someone's loft, or a trunk, for a century or two.

Jacaranda flicked the table light on. She glanced up at Déraciné. He sat impassive in the chair, overhanging it, bulky and tall.

She ran her hands over the plates, over the binding. It was undeniably authentic, and yet –

Jacaranda shook her head. 'I give up. It is a very impressive fake.'

Déraciné snorted. 'The book is authentic. You know it's authentic.'

Jacaranda scowled. 'It is an elaborate joke. Pointless, and probably costly, but to what end I don't know. The 'Xenology Codex'? There's no such book.'

The spirit of a smile touched Déraciné's lips. 'And yet what do you hold in your hands? The 'Xenology Codex'. The ancient manuscript detailing alien life and cultures. I would have thought you would have understood the value of this manuscript. You, above all else.'

She stared at him. There was something of the operatic villain about him – she almost expected him to produce a white, half-face mask. His beard was elegantly combed. His moustache twirled. His eyes were dark blue, almost purple, and seemed old. Older than the rest of him. She'd have guessed his age somewhere between the sixties and seventies. It was a dreadful thought. She was the wrong side of forty.

Jacaranda sat back in the chair, running fingers through her hair. The sides were razored short. The top flopped over them, all scarecrow spikes and fringe. The gloss black of her youth was streaked with silver. Her fingers were lean, unadorned save for the black diamond rings Henghist had given her for their engagement and wedding.

'Mr Déraciné.' She shook her head. 'This is a very complex and clever fake. I should know; I've been a bookseller for too many years and I've seen any number of manuscripts purporting to be in Jesus' handwriting, or the diary of Jack the Ripper, or with Robin Hood's mark. But this?' She lifted the heavy codex. 'A four hundred year old guide to alien races? Please. Attempt something believable next time.'

He stood up abruptly. She was tall, but he was taller and much broader and the room was small, little more than a broom cupboard. 'You do not believe me?'

'Alien life?' she snorted. 'Life is strange enough, but little green men? UFO's over Salisbury Hill? Try a new-age shop. They might be gullible enough.'

Déraciné shook his head. 'I came here in good faith. I was told this was The Bookshop.'

He stressed the 'the', his accent slipping, changing. Definitely not a local boy she thought. No trace of a Berkshire accent.

'It is. I am. This is the best bookshop for miles around. There are charity bookshops,' she shrugged, 'but they're no competition.'

Déraciné inclined his head. 'In that case I will leave you. I apologise for taking up your time.'

He was out the door and gone in an instant. Jacaranda closed her eyes. Why do all the idiots beat a path to my door? It's not like I haven't enough –

She flicked her eyes open and stared at the desk. The codex sat on it mutely, forgotten. She shook her head, getting to her feet and picking it up. It was heavier than she'd expected. She cradled it to her chest, pushing the door open with her foot.

Courtney was on the till. Miles was stocking up; it was only his second day. And Déraciné was closing the inner door behind him.

Jacaranda ran through the shop. It smelt of everything homely – dust and age and books and bookworms.

She caught the door as it closed. The outer door was closing.

'Déraciné.'

She caught the outer door. Pulled it open after him.

It was dark outside. Wrongly dark. The darkness was solid, closed off, all consuming.

Déraciné stood with arms folded, watching her. He was more real than the darkness.

She blinked, staring. She held the codex in one hand, the door in the other. There was light behind her but it didn't spill across the doorway.

'Welcome to my world.'

He was reaching for her. The codex was too heavy: she was about to drop it. She abandoned the door to grasp the book. Déraciné lifted her; pulled her out of the doorway.

He was far stronger than he looked. She twisted, trying to pull out of his grip but he merely turned her round, set her feet on the ground.

'Look.'

The doorway – her bookshop doorway – hung in the darkness. Pale yellow light filled it, diminishing as the outer door swung to.

'No. You can't. I –'

He held her tight, painfully immobile. The door closed but didn't vanish. Remained where it was, incongruous.

'Where am I? What's going on?'

'This is my world.' His voice was softer, sibilant. 'That is your bookshop, is it not?'

Jacaranda nodded. 'What –'

He shook her effortlessly. 'If that is your bookshop, then I find you guilty of genocide.'

She managed to twist around. 'What the –'

He was no longer holding her. The back of his hand caught her cheek: sent her tumbling. She cried out, trying to break her fall, tasting blood in her mouth.

The ground was cold. And solid. She shifted, feeling its clammy texture.

Déraciné was beside her in an instant, drawing her up into a seated position. She tried to bat his hands away, but she might as well have tried to push a building over with one finger.

'I am sorry.' His voice was harsher, colder. 'I lost my wife to your world. Your bookshop. It consumed them all.'

Jacaranda shook her head: only her cheek stung: she could feel the blood on it. 'I don't know what the hell you're talking about.'

Déraciné gave a short, bark-like laugh. 'You don't? You admit to owning the bookshop though.'

She nodded. Her cheek no longer stung; it felt numb. 'It's my shop.'

He let her go and moved away. She swayed but didn't fall.

'Once all this was mountains. Blue grey heights capped in snow. Crystal clear skies. Ridge after ridge, lost in the mist and heat hazes.'

Jacaranda could see nothing but the shop door. Where the display window was – should have been – was only solid darkness. She shifted over. The doorway was a couple of metres away. *If I can get to it –*

His hand grabbed her hair and jerked her backwards.

Jacaranda screamed as she fell. Déraciné caught her hands and pinned them to her sides.

'You know,' he shook his head. 'I actually believe you when you say you don't know. That's what makes it tragic.'

Her head was throbbing. He knelt over her, obscuring the doorway. 'Someone close to you – someone you trust – has lied to you. Consistently and deliberately.'

She started to shake her head but stopped at the pain. 'No.' *Why is my voice so weak? So powerless. Henghist would not lie to me. We have no secrets. Not after twenty-five years of marriage. I know all his dark family secrets. I was at Horsa's marriage. His suicide was a shock. But the disappearance of his daughter – and what was his wife's name?*

'What do you know of string theory, dark matter and the Big Bang theory?'

Jacaranda snorted. 'I'm a bookseller, not a physicist.'

Déraciné scowled, shaking his head. 'Some of your leading scientists now believe that there are alternate earths, and that the collision of two of these parallel earths led to the Big Bang.'

She frowned. 'What's all this got to do with you kidnapping me?'

Déraciné held up his hand to forestall her. 'It is happening again. Alternate earths are,' – he snorted. 'Well, not colliding, but being drawn into this one. And,' he shuddered, shaking his head.

'What?' Jacaranda managed.

He looked at her, his eyes almost black. 'And sooner or later, this bookshop will precipitate another Big Bang.'

Jacaranda shook her head. 'No. Not my bookshop. You're talking –' she stopped, feeling dizzy as pain rolled through her.

Déraciné sighed. 'Alternate realities exist. There might even be one where none of this had to happen.'

Jacaranda swallowed. Her throat was dry. And I thought the hardest thing I'd have to do today was get used to the idea of having two members of staff in. 'None of what?' she whispered.

Déraciné hauled himself to his feet. 'You do not believe. You do not accept that this is real. I am sorry, but you have to understand that this is very real.'

He turned and headed for the door. Jacaranda rolled onto her side, gritting her teeth, and stood up.

The door was closing. Déraciné was inside. He gave her a friendly little wave.

Jacaranda crossed to the door, so strange, so real, amongst the solid darkness. It refused to budge. She pushed. Pulled. It didn't move.

'Come on.' She hammered on the glass pane.

It made no sound, though she knew she'd touched the glass. The lobby was hazy, vague. She could see both doors, but no further in. She felt something in her pocket: pulled out the door key.

It turned in the lock, but the door refused to budge. It wasn't that it was wedged shut. The door simply wouldn't open.

Jacaranda sighed, running her fingers through her hair again. Her scalp was still sore from where Déraciné had pulled her. The blood on her cheek had dried. She put the key back in her pocket. Tried half-heartedly opening it.

'Open sesame.' Pushing, pulling it, made no difference.

She looked back into the darkness. It lacked depth. She took a half step. Tripped over something.

Jacaranda sprawled in the darkness. She twisted round, rubbing her ankle. The 'Xenology Codex' lay forgotten where she'd dropped it. She pulled it to her. It seemed heavier. She snorted. Or I'm getting weaker.

The only light was from the door, and that was barely enough to read by. She didn't like sitting with her back to it, but managed to wedge herself into an almost corner, cradling the codex on her thighs.

Twenty-five years of marriage. I knew Henghist a little, before we were married. She frowned. We met at a disco. He just seemed – right. She smiled.

He'd proposed not long after she'd shown him her bookshop. He'd had suggestions for how she could improve it; contacts who had supplied her, through him, with all the art, religious and poetry books she could sell.

He'd taken care of everything for her so she could concentrate on The Bookshop. Wrapped in his arms she felt safe. Secure. He was, she supposed, a house husband, though she'd never asked if that was all he wanted.

He'd cooked and cleaned the house they shared. She had to do nothing at home except the shop accounts if she didn't want to. She'd wanted to give him a child – that was what he wanted almost more than her. But it was the one thing that she hadn't been able to give him.

She looked up, the codex open but unread. This is mad. I'm mad. Henghist loves me. He wouldn't –

She twisted the engagement ring.

He changed his name for you, a little voice in her head said. At times he'd looked a little strangely at you, like you didn't understand something, even though your IQ was over one-fourty. And there was always something about him when he was with Horsa, some little family secret that you weren't part of.

13

She shook her head, looking into the impenetrable darkness. 'But what is all this? Illusion? Hypnotism. A dream.' She pinched herself. Winced.

Movement distracted her and she turned. Lights were going off within. She pushed the codex aside and stood up, hammering on the glass, shaking the door.

'Miles. Miles! Courtney. Can you hear me?'

Her staff went past, locking up for the evening.

They disappeared through the stockroom door. The light was gone. Only the security light in the lobby.

Jacaranda shivered. The darkness became cold. She rattled the door, but to no avail. Her breath hung in the darkness. Goose bumps crawled over her skin.

The stockroom door opened and her staff emerged into the lobby.

'Miles. Courtney.' She pushed on the door. Slapped the glass with her hand.

She could see them clearly. Miles was checking the internal door. Courtney checked the stockroom door. Both turned to leave –

Jacaranda stared. The door hadn't opened but the lobby was empty. They'd gone. Somehow. Somewhere. She tried one last time before sliding down, huddling into a corner.

She tucked her knees into her chest. Wrapped her arms round. It was summer. It had been. Wherever – here – was, it was the depth of winter. She pressed her face against her knees, trying to curl up as tightly as possible.

Her ankles were cold. One was throbbing. Her toes became blocks of ice. Her neck was cold. The ice was advancing across her shoulders and back. Her arms were cold. Her fingers were numb. The cold was seeping inside her clothes, inside her skin.

Jacaranda retreated into herself. There was a pit of warmth in her stomach. So much to do with Henghist. Their first time, that night, after the disco. Their wedding. Holidaying in Barbados – she tried to remember what it was like, the feel of sun on her skin. They'd not holidayed for two years. Christmas in front of a real log fire. Waking up, so many times, in Henghist's arms, safe and warm and snug.

There was warmth out there. Beyond the tunnel. It was melting her resistance. She just had to come back. Leave her memories behind and return to the present.

The coldness was dissipating. Warmth was seeping in, and water.

Jacaranda gave a start. She was lying in a puddle from the ice that had melted off her. She sat up slowly.

She was wrapped in a towel, in the stockroom of her bookshop. There were gaps of cooler air. Déraciné was pointedly looking away.

Jacaranda realised she was near naked beneath the towel and clutched it tighter. 'What?' she managed, her jaw aching, her throat raw and cold.

She tried to cough but there was nothing there. It wasn't exactly warm, but it certainly wasn't freezing either.

'Where?'

He turned back, studying her face. 'This is your shop. Your time. Your world.'

She shook her head. Her cheek was raw icy pain. 'Where – how?'

Déraciné shook his head. 'I showed you my world. The scientists who postulated there were countless billion alternate realities were wrong. There are only a few.'

'Did you –' she licked her lips. 'Where are my clothes?'

He pointed to a chair beside the table. Her clothes were slung over the back, dripping. The chair stood in a large puddle.

'I didn't want you to freeze. I wanted you to realise –' he paused, an impenetrable look crossing his face, 'what is happening.'

She frowned. 'What? Realise what?'

Déraciné shook his head. 'The worlds that have fallen are like moths around your light. We are drawn in, and when the light goes, we freeze.'

She curled her legs beneath her, drawing the towel tighter. 'I didn't do it. I don't know who – or how – or what –'

'I know.' Déraciné was nodding. 'This bookshop is a lodestone.' He smiled. 'Time is a wave. The right person, at the right place, can ride the course of history. This bookshop is the moon, pulling the tides out of pattern, out of order, out of time.'

'Jacaranda!'

Henghist was racing across the stockroom, shock and concern on his face.

Déraciné tipped his hat to her. 'I will leave you now your husband is here to look after you. One thing, my cornix sinistra,' and his eyes gleamed with humour as Henghist wrapped her in his arms, 'take a look at the title page of the codex.'

Déraciné was going. Henghist was asking questions, fussing. It would have been easy to close her eyes, to let him take care of her, let him take care of the arrangements as he'd always done –

Something slotted into place. He'd always done everything for her. Even gone in after she got home and tidied the shop up for her. And occasionally dropped books off from his contacts, but always out of hours. He had access to the shop. If – whatever I experienced – wasn't an illusion –

She slipped an arm round Henghist's shoulders to hug him and flipped the codex open with her other hand.

'The Xenology Codex,' the title page proudly read, 'written by Henghist Goring and Horsa Streatley.'

Jacaranda stared. The alien book, the ancient manuscript about alien worlds and civilisations, had been written by her husband.

Four hundred years ago.

Hashishim, Inc.

Wizerbowski raised the rifle. It was almost too easy.

He was in the south of France, twenty-five years previous. It had been identified as the best time and place to eliminate the target.

In his sights he could see the target family's tent. In addition to the target there was his sister and their parents. They were not to be harmed: collateral damage was sloppy. Horsa would skin him for sloppy work.

He frowned. There was no need for the job: it was satisfying Horsa's personal wish for revenge. It was petty. Unbecoming for an officer of the Hashishim. But he had to remain trusted. Horsa had to remain under surveillance.

The campsite was near the ocean: an ideal tourist spot. The death would damage their reputation, but Wizerbowski had no problems with that. The time lines would merge, blend again, soon enough after the disposal.

A figure came out of the tent. Wizerbowski's finger tightened on the trigger. It was the father. He relaxed.

He caressed the stock of the rifle. It had only one projectile, but that was all he needed. All he'd ever needed.

The tent flap moved again. The sister.

'Come on kid,' he muttered. 'Get to the beach. Think of the French babes.'

The sun beat down. It was early morning on a gloriously sunny day. A day to be up and about. The records might imply the target had historical proclivities as opposed to an appreciation of beach time, but there was definitely an awareness of the wonderfulness of nature. The target should be out in the sun, heading for some ancient gîte or church, camera in hand.

'Come on, Courtney. Come enjoy the last day of your life.'

His finger tightened on the trigger as the tent breathed, as the canvas spilled apart and the boy emerged. Wizerbowski fired.

The projectile was near instantaneous. Speed of light technology. No ugly cartridges to punch holes in the target, to leave behind absolute proof of assassination. Blood was sloppy.

The projectile honed in on the target – and failed.

Wizerbowski stared. There had been a trace of movement beyond the visual. The sights would have recorded it automatically. The target should be dead – but he had left the tent area now, dressed for a day exploring the nearby town.

Wizerbowski cursed. The projectiles were infallible. It was impossible for them to fail. Yet it had failed.

He stood up, dusting himself down as he dismantled the rifle. It was time to be gone. Time to finish what he'd begun.

It was easy enough to slip back into the present, into headquarters, to find the next recommended point of delivery. The butterfly gave him full access, but it wouldn't do to be caught by Horsa until he'd completed the termination. Whatever had happened to the projectile could be examined later. The sights had almost unlimited storage capacities: he'd investigate at his ease, when the target was removed from the present.

Wizerbowski slipped out of the building as rapidly as he'd returned. He had the details of the next most suitable transaction point and two projectiles; a pistol for each.

He stepped into a darkened alleyway, tugged his sleeve up – and emerged in an unlit train passage. The noise was thunderous – the steam train was following the Rhine, chuntering along at high speed with typical Teutonic efficiency.

It was twenty-eight years previous. The target had only his father this time with him, a long weekend paid for by the father's employer.

I take it Horsa has had the parents, the family, checked out. He scowled at the fräulein in the serving car.

The target becomes an integral part; must therefore be removed before he can become that.

Wizerbowski was used to Horsa's shotgun approach to speaking, but even so he knew his boss was rattled. Something wasn't quite going to plan. Revenge wasn't tasting as sweet as it was expected to.

If he'd been stupid, he'd have asked his boss why they didn't simply take out the head of the bookshop. Instead of targeting her staff, simply kill –

His thoughts blanched and he stumbled, masking it as the train began to curve. They didn't use the K word. They removed. They eliminated. They altered. They didn't K.

Now I'm getting rattled.

He entered the dining car and halted. Every eye in the place turned to look at him. He scowled, thankful the pistols were tucked in the back of his belt, hidden behind the leather coat.

'You never seen a black man before?'

The diners, for the most part stodgy Aryans, looked away, horrified. A woman with a feathered hat sniffed loudly, tucking in to an expensive confection of cream, butter, jam and sugar.

'This is the eighties, love. Enjoy it before it's over.'

She looked up at him, cream and jam on her fat lips, a terrified look in her porcine eyes.

He moved past her, his boots thudding as the other diners concentrated on their meals.

'I have. Seen a black man before, I mean. I was –'

21

Wizerbowski looked at the speaker, freezing his expression. It was the target's father, still looking like he belonged in the seventies, with his sideburns and the distasteful orange and brown suit that had never really been fashionable.

'Oh,' he managed to say, pausing.

The man nodded. 'Pakistan. Worked with a group of engineers. Bloody hard workers – oh,' he glanced at his son.

Wizerbowski looked at the target. The boy was staring out of the window, rapt. Dark woodlands filled the far bank of the Rhine. Wizerbowski tried not to shudder. Trees had always unnerved him.

The target had thick national health glasses. Messy hair. Hand me down clothes. There was nothing special about him. Nothing to warrant Horsa's desire for revenge.

Wizerbowski shook himself. That was dangerous thinking. The target was simply the target. Morals had very little to do with it.

The target's father coughed. 'Will you join me?' He grinned, lowering his voice. 'What you said to that woman. Did me good to hear. Strutting about, just because she's wealthy. She's German,' he hissed. Lowering his voice still further. 'When we had an empire we gave it away, fairly peacefully. We didn't invade –'

Wizerbowski grinned. 'That's not what they say in Belfast.'

The target's father's expression closed.

He resisted the temptation to click his heels together, and carried on down the carriage.

Do not interact. Do not become involved. Do not interfere.

Horsa's imperative buzzed in his head. Now I know the target's father. He will remember me if anything happens. She will; that fat German woman.

The target is still a problem. Wizerbowski ground his teeth together. I could simply go back in there. Draw the pistols and fire. He shook his head. It would be too unusual. A boy dying from wasp stings in a closed compartment after a black man fires pistols at him. It would be remembered. Investigated. He scowled. It would be like dropping a boulder in one of Horsa's beloved time streams.

He moved down the corridor until he found a window he could open. He tugged his sleeve up – and emerged back in the alleyway beside the office.

He took the back stairs, climbing to the fifth floor. The server room was deserted as usual as he typed his request into the laptop. The details came back in moments. A third time and place to erase the target before he could achieve his dangerous potential.

'Wizerbowski.'

He whirled round. Horsa stood behind him. The door was still closed.

'No doubt you wish to explain.'

Wizerbowski waited for more, but his boss just glowered. 'The target – there were complications.'

Horsa snorted. 'You've got two Impossible pistols. An Impossible rifle. How could a rifleman, particularly one of your calibre –' he snorted, wheezing for a moment, 'require a second, let alone a third?'

'The rifle,' – he'd not handed it in yet for examination of the sights' ultra visual record, '– the projectile failed.'

He tossed the rifle to Horsa.

His boss scowled. 'The technology doesn't fail. That's why they're Impossible. If you've been sloppy –'

'Check the record. While you're doing that –'

Horsa raised the rifle then lowered it, disbelief on his face. 'You're right.' He frowned. 'The sights verify, but I'll need to check.'

Wizerbowski froze. The quantum butterfly gave him full access to the organisation's abilities, but there were rumours about Horsa. He only needed to expose his arm to fresh air, but Horsa –

It was said, whispered, in Braille, far from wherever Horsa was, that his butterfly was the size of his back. If it gave him the ability to freeze or bend time at will –

'Try again.' Horsa was studying him. 'Take him out of the equation. This town has a million souls but most are not a target. He is. Remove him.'

Wizerbowski checked the coordinates and ran.

In the sunlight the butterfly burned for an instant and then he was standing on a mountainside far away, thirty-one years previous.

Jagged, snow covered peaks surrounded him. He was high, high above the plains and it was crystal bright: crystal cold.

He looked around. A dam blocked a distant valley, the sunlight shimmering on its surface.

'He worked with engineers.'

Wizerbowski grinned. He was far in the target's past. The target would only be five or six, and easy prey to the toxin of an Impossible wasp. Better still, it was an undeveloped country. Strange things happened all the time. The boy would cease to exist and that would please Horsa. That was the overriding concern. For the greater good.

On a distant hilltop a group of people had gathered. The dam was a recent construct: Pakistani workforce, British design and architect, funding by the World Bank.

The target would be there with his family. Wizerbowski drew the pistols. They were keyed to the target. There would be no misses.

It would seem, simply, as if two small wasps had stung him. Speech would go instantaneously. Then his heart would speed up. He'd twitch and rave silently, foam at the mouth like a rabid dog and then die. A bad day for the Tarbela dam project perhaps, but a good day for Horsa. For his own survival, Wizerbowski needed Horsa to have a good day. He aimed at the distant group.

'You will not succeed.'

He whirled around, firing one of the pistols automatically. The miniature wasp left the pistol at the speed of light. And died instantly.

Wizerbowski stared.

A short figure, swathed in thick woollen robes was watching him. Their face was hidden. There was something; a nuance, a lilt, to the voice. It wasn't Western, but it was westernised.

'Who are you?'

They chuckled. He knew then that it was a woman.

'I am a protector. You cannot harm the one I guard. Because I am here, neither you nor any of your compatriots succeed.'

Wizerbowski scowled. 'You stopped the wasp in the south of France.'

The woman nodded. She appeared unarmed, but the fact she'd stopped an Impossible wasp – in itself an impossibility –

'What is the boy to you?'

She chuckled. 'Courtney is the one I guard. I am with him everywhere. Know that because I am here, your attempts have failed. Save yourself the effort. Return, now.'

Wizerbowski shook his head. 'The target is too important. Horsa will –' he broke off, staring into the depths of the hood. 'You are one of them.' He frowned. 'What have you done to displease Horsa?'

She laughed, and there was a delicious chiming sound to it. 'Nothing. But I am of Courtney. I will stop you because I have. Because I have, he does – what he does – and here I am.'

He shook his head. 'You speak in riddles.'

She seemed to shrug. 'We are who we are made and who we make ourselves.'

He raised the remaining pistol. 'I will shoot you.'

She shook her head; he could just see the points of light reflecting in her eyes, impossibly green despite her Asian accent. 'You will shoot and the wasp will die for nothing.'

'How do you travel?'

She chuckled. 'I am where he is. I am his protection, his salvation, and his greatest achievement.'

Wizerbowski fired.

The wasp burst, like sunlight, out of the barrel.

The woman held her hand up.

It blurred through the air, falling to the ground at her feet.

She sighed. Her fingers were lean; light brown and unadorned but perfectly human. He had been wondering: anyone who could anger Horsa so could be so much more than human.

'Go. Take what you know. We will, no doubt, meet again.'

He scowled, retrieving the other pistol and tucking both into his belt. 'If I fail, another will try.'

She paced towards him and he found he couldn't move, caught by the pull of her eyes.

One of her hands gripped his wrist, the other his sleeve.

'You will find there are greater problems than the one I protect.'

So near, she smelt exotic and strange. Jasmine and orange blossom and something, something he couldn't identify.

'If not him, there are others Horsa will go after,' he taunted.

She tore his sleeve up. His last memory was of her chuckling as he was drawn back, back to his present.

Henghist Road

I was there, the first time that Henghist came to our world uninvited. A pair of Irregulars, the Committee's Peace Keepers, ushered him into my mistress' tent.

It was obvious he wasn't from our world. He stared at my mistress coldly, ignoring the Peace Keepers. At a sign from my mistress they retreated, leaving us alone with him.

He was an older man than me, though I was not a man then. He was a student by his age I would have guessed, though the look in his eyes was of an older man. Still, if the Oracle had dismissed the Peace Keepers, there was nothing to fear.

'Are you the one to explain all this?' he demanded.

'All what?' my mistress asked, sipping her tea.

'All this,' Henghist repeated, waving his arms about. 'I was just in Reading. And then –'

My mistress put her tea cup down. 'The town you were born in is not called Reading. You were born on another world. There was an explosion. The town was abandoned but the effects of the bomb and its conjunction with the portal caused the destruction to continue year upon year. In time your world will be destroyed. You came through the doorway – what your people call the heart of destruction – to see what lies beyond it. But that is not what brings you here.'

Henghist was staring, eyes narrowed. 'Do you think –'

My mistress sighed patiently. 'You are far from home. The world you found is too similar – and so dissimilar – from your own. You found something that's changed what you expected.'

Henghist nodded, sinking to his knees. At a look from the Oracle I poured him a cup of tea and passed it over. He took it without looking at me and sipped it.

'An opportunity. This crack, whatever it is, leads into other worlds, other possibilities. Horsa's having a field day. We can visit these worlds, exploit them, take from them. But there's this woman. Little more than a girl, really. Jacaranda. She's the owner of the bookshop where the portal – whatever it is – opens. She's –' he shrugged, shaking his head.

'Do you find her interesting?' my mistress asked, a half smile on her lips.

Henghist scowled. 'She's an easy lay. So – unquestioning,' he said, glancing at me for the first time. 'But –'

The Oracle looked at me. I scurried over with more tea. She took a sip, and patted my head, and I returned to my corner.

'But what?'

Henghist tilted his head a little, narrowing his gaze. 'You know what this portal is. What it can do. I have seen that as well. I can make very good use of it. But Jacaranda's in the way.'

My mistress shook her head. 'Think of her as an accoutrement. She comes with the bookshop.'

Henghist scowled. 'What am I supposed to do with her? She'll figure something is up.'

The Oracle shook her head. 'No. Keep her close. Keep her distracted. Marry her.'

He raised an eyebrow. 'Marry the girl? No. She's good for a quick fuck in a –'

'Do not swear in front of one of my orphans. Please, Henghist. Business is business but I will not tolerate unwarranted crudeness.'

He scowled. 'What is she, then, that I must marry her?'

The Oracle looked over at me and smiled, a little sadly I thought. 'Think of her as an orphan. She needs someone to care for her. Protect her. Shelter her. Take everything she offers but tell her none of this.'

He shrugged. 'I'll think about it.' He frowned. 'I know what the doorway – portal – whatever – does, but not how or why. Is this another world?'

My mistress took a sip of her tea. 'This is Earth. Every decision is a possibility. Every possibility exists in an alternate version of the original. Mostly the realities mesh, but there are always alternates.'

'Is this the original or is my world – my,' he frowned, 'reality, the original?'

She smiled. 'The Reading you found, that is the original. The bookshop at the heart of the realities.' She shook her head. 'It's – capabilities – are unknown, save to a very few.'

'And Jacaranda runs the bookshop. If we were to be partnered –'

The Oracle nodded. 'There is more though. Realities will blend into one another if there are too many cracks. You can help prevent it. Help prevent Armageddon, the end of everything.'

He frowned. 'On my world –'

'You cannot stop what is happening to your world.'

Henghist looked up sharply. 'But –'

'But you can slow it down. Hold off the inevitable. Do not, whatever you do, let Jacaranda become aware of this. She will not understand.'

He shrugged. 'I can keep her busy. What Jacaranda doesn't know won't detract from her bearing my line. And while she's doing that,' he chuckled.

'Thank you for your time.' He stood up and was gone in an instant, the tent flap snapping behind him.

I looked at my mistress. She looked thoughtful.

'Mohan,' she said after a while, 'I may need you to warn the Hashishim.'

--

I was there, the second time that Henghist came to our world, to our version of the earth that he had migrated to.

31

He was accompanied by Wizerbowski, one of the Hashishim. The Hashishim had a fearsome reputation, but he had made a point of always thanking me for the tea.

'Why am I here?' Henghist demanded, wrenching his arm out of Wizerbowski's grip. 'You risked everything by sending this thug –'

'You may leave us, Wizerbowski,' my mistress said sharply, then softened her tone. 'I will speak to you later.'

He nodded and withdrew, making a face at Henghist's back and winking at me on the way out.

'You said –'

'What do you know of the quantum butterfly and the Impossible wasp?'

Henghist stared blankly. 'I have no idea what you're talking about.'

My mistress nodded slowly. 'I am almost certain you are telling the truth. The world of the quantum butterfly is gone. Destroyed. Pulled into the orbit of another reality and crushed.'

He stared, eyes wide. 'What? How? What –'

The Oracle waved away his questions. 'The Impossible wasps are being harvested. Their poison is incredibly effective.' She half smiled. 'Impossibly effective. If it is not you –'

'It's not Jacaranda.'

She nodded. 'Of course not. You are not foolish enough to have told her any of this. How is she?'

Henghist sneered 'We've been married for eleven years. She doesn't know of the portal. She's more interested in her old books and her own pleasure than –'

'Has she conceived?'

Henghist's look darkened. 'No. No matter what we try she can't conceive. During her most fertile times,' he glanced over at me and shook his head. 'It's not for young ears.'

He frowned. 'There was a kid last time.' His gaze swung back to my mistress. 'You haven't changed either. How?'

The Oracle shook her head. 'The portal is being used too much. Realities are being harvested. If not by you, then –'

'Horsa.'

She nodded. 'He endangers everyone. All realities. Deny him access or other realities will fall.'

Henghist scowled. 'He is my only contact with my world. I can't talk to my wife – how could I?'

'Do you love Jacaranda –'

He snorted. 'Love's got nothing to do with this,' he snapped. 'Once she's six months pregnant I might tell her, but not till then. Horsa,' he scowled. 'He's always boasting about his daughter Bridget. How clever she is. How sensitive she is.'

'Do not even joke of telling her, Henghist. This is serious.'

He scowled. 'She's – what? An orphan girl. No wonder she never speaks of her family. She likes books. I will admit, in the sack, she's a goer, but –'

'Do what you want with Jacaranda,' my mistress hissed, 'but never tell her. But you must stop Horsa.'

'What's so special about Jac?'

My mistress shook her head. 'If you do not stop your own brother, I will have him stopped. By the Hashishim.'

Henghist stared. 'You – what are you playing at? You give me free rein to harvest the realities then ask me to rein Horsa in –'

'Think how your brother will feel when you deny him.'

Henghist stared at my mistress. There was a moment's silence. Then he nodded curtly. 'I know what to do. I can see myself out of your reality.'

'Mohan,' she said after a few moments thought, 'please fetch Wizerbowski. I may have need of him.'

33

I shivered as I went out, glad the Hashishim wasn't being summoned for me, and a little scared, and sorry, for this Jacaranda.

--

I was there, the third time Henghist came to our reality.

'What do you want?' he snapped. 'I stopped my brother –'

He was older. Far longer had passed in the second interval than the first.

'And you have taken over yourself. Worlds have fallen to your greed, Henghist. You strip the worlds of resources, of minerals –'

He shrugged. 'Why not? There are new alternates being created all the time. Better I do it than anyone else.'

'Better?' the Oracle echoed. 'You own world rushes to termination. Once there are no alternates progress will halt. The world will stagnate, regress, collapse. Then –'

'Then what?' he demanded. 'I cannot save my home world. I have no offspring – no matter what I do, Jacaranda doesn't conceive. She's older now, older than I wanted her to be when she bore my first child. I can't turn to Horsa.' He glanced at me, scowling. 'He's committed suicide. His precious, special, daughter has disappeared. If I can't have what I want, why shouldn't I rush to Armageddon?'

My mistress was staring at him. Something he'd said she hadn't known. That surprised me. She knew about the portal way before any other dweller in any reality discovered it. She knew what would and what might happen before it did – except now she didn't.

'Horsa's dead?' she asked softly.

Henghist scowled. 'I should never have listened to you. I've lost my brother and I've lost my world and if I can't get my wife pregnant I might as well fuck her to Armageddon and take all this with me.'

He broke off, his anger frozen, as a scimitar blade touched his throat.

'You do not insult the Oracle. You are nothing in this world, Incomer.'

The Janissary officer had stepped silently into the tent. Her eyes were blue-purple.

I quailed. Wizerbowski did not scare me personally, but she did. It was true there had been a slow trickle of Incomers, people who'd accidentally crossed into our reality, but the captain's way of dealing with it was an overreaction. Not that I'd have dared speak in her presence. I was only one of the Oracle's orphan boys, a messenger, tea maker, or whatever else she asked of me.

'Captain. Let Henghist speak. You overreact.'

The captain scowled, lowering her sword but not sheathing it, taking a half step to one side, ready to interpose her body or slay Henghist as his actions demanded.

Henghist glowered at the Oracle. 'My wife knows. Someone from another world told her, threw her into the dark of his desolate, disintegrating world.' He shook his head. 'I flung the exile through the portal but she knows.' He sighed heavily. 'She still trusts me, mostly.' A wolfish look came into his eyes. 'She cannot stop me. Once she is out of the way –'

'You cannot kill your wife.' I burst out, then stopped, horrified at my presumption.

The captain was staring at me with cold eyes. I felt like I was on the block and the blade was already descending.

'I won't,' the Incomer said, turning back to face my mistress. 'She'll die in an alternate reality, or be trapped. She's too innocent. And if she can't conceive, what's her use to me?'

The Oracle shook her head. 'This world is closed to you, Henghist. I will not fetch you here again and do not return. Any Incomers will be dealt with by the captain. I suggest you do what you can to slow down the approaching Armageddon.'

He snorted. 'I'll do what I want. I've got nothing to gain.'

'But everything to lose, Henghist. There is still hope –'

He scowled, shaking his head. 'Do not try anything. The ways of my adopted world –' and he looked round the tent, sneering, 'are a lot more developed than yours.'

He turned and stalked out. The captain followed him two paces behind. As she left Wizerbowski came in, unrolling his sleeve.

'Wizerbowski. Henghist is to be watched. He is the primary threat. I know I cannot give you orders, but the Hashishim –'

He nodded smoothly, grinning. 'When Armageddon comes –'

She nodded. 'Do not tell me. He is still Jacaranda's husband. Do not move against him. I do not want her hurt.'

Wizerbowski nodded and withdrew.

'Oracle, I'm sorry –'

'Hush, Mohan,' she said, waving away my apology. 'I wondered how long you could keep silent for.'

'Oracle,' I asked nervously, 'can you tell me how you know about his wife. About Jacaranda.'

My mistress laughed. 'Of course I can, Mohan, but not today. It is a tale for another time.'

Bridge of Souls

'Won't you take my hand?'

James shook his head. 'I don't think that would be very wise of me now, do you?'

Bridge shook her head, sinking back into the chair. James faced her across the desk, her desk, where she interviewed potential clients. He sat next to the door, not that it helped: her PA had let James in on his way out, and would be gone for several hours.

'So you're the famous Bridget?'

'Bridge,' she answered automatically, then, seeing his look, added, 'everyone calls me Bridge.'

James wore a pale green shirt, open necked, no tie, and a black business jacket. He wore a single ring on his right hand, a claddagh, heart pointing inwards. He was early forties, Bridge guessed, with a plain, if somewhat babyishly soft face; no beard. His clothes were clean, his hair was tidy and she could still smell the aftershave on his cheeks.

'You know who I am, don't you?'

Bridge nodded, her mouth dry. Her hands were clammy. Her stomach knotted. James sat opposite her coolly, the slightest trace of a Northern Irish burr to his voice.

'You've been looking for me, haven't you?'

Bridge looked away –

--

'So. You've info for us. You won't tell us how you got it. You say things –' DI Gray scowled, exasperated. 'You know things only the murderer would know. But your alibi is unbreakable.'

'I came to you. I can help. I know things –'

DI Gray slammed a file onto the table, making her start. 'I don't believe it. There's no way. No way,' he enunciated slowly, 'you could know this. If you're not the murderer –' and the dark haired policeman scowled – 'and I can't prove that yet, that leaves two options. The murderer's accomplice or a team member.'

Bridge shook her head. 'No. I can't say. You wouldn't believe me.'

Gray got up, wheeled about, hands clasped behind his back. 'I know you. Oh, your type. Though you are the most unusual I've seen.'

Bridge leant forwards. 'Yes?'

He turned back to face her. 'You've a loose screw. Something, up here.' He waggled his fingers by his head. 'I thought you were real. I bought the business suit. The hair, the nails, the dainty heels.' He moved to the door of the room.

'No. Detective Inspector Gray, trust me. I'm not what –'

'Interview terminated twenty-two thirty-seven.'

The uniformed police officer sitting in clicked off the tape recorder.

'Constable. Give Miss Bridget a biscuit and get her out of here. I've got a murderer to catch. I don't need –'

'Nikoletta.' Bridge stood up. 'You don't believe me, fine. But look into a Nikoletta Smith, Estonian. She married an Englishman. She's dead now.'

'And what would you know –'

--

Bridge looked back at James. 'The Police are investigating. I gave them Nikoletta. Did you know she dreams of death houses?'

James tugged at his jacket sleeves. Knocked some dust away. 'You know you can't play the psychologist with me, don't you?'

Bridge nodded. 'I know. I just wondered why. The urge to kill, beyond self-preservation. Where does it come into fight or flight?'

'You think I'm going to explain myself to you?'

38

Bridge clamped her knees together to stop her legs from shaking. 'As you've come here.' She stared down at the desk for a moment. It smelt of old leather and alcohol. She scrunched her fingers into a fist. She could almost smell the vintage of the whiskey.

'You know who I am.' She looked up at James. 'You know I know what you've done.'

James chuckled. 'And you think I'll tell you as a prelude to murdering you?'

Her leg spasmed. 'I think you want to boast. The only thing I don't know –'

James chuckled, leaning back in the chair. 'What don't you know?'

She shook her head. She couldn't get past him. Wouldn't get out the door. Even if she did, there was no one in the house. 'How,' she asked, bracing herself, 'are you going to do it? It won't look like an accident. And the Police know –'

James held his hand up and she stopped. 'There are higher authorities.'

She stared, feeling the growing need to relieve herself.

'That stopped you, didn't it?'

Bridge nodded dumbly. Something he'd said; something he'd done.

'Did you know I had you investigated before I came here?'

She shook her head.

James smiled the smile of a proud father. 'You're very interesting, Bridge. Hard to track at times. A double first from Cambridge. A public breakdown. Run-ins with the Police. Visits to The Priory and other establishments.' He leaned forwards, elbows on the desk, fingers steepled. 'An addictive personality, am I right?'

She nodded, cold despite the warmth of the room.

'Do you think your mother would be proud of you?'

Bridge shivered, feeling the goose bumps break out on her arms. She flinched, remembering cold beds and being thrashed for lying; being thrashed for having an overactive imagination.

'And here you are,' James continued, James the murderer, James who she'd been tracking the progress of, James whom her PA had let into her house. 'Working from home? Some kind of grief counselling? Does it pay well? What's the pay like?' he pressed on relentlessly. 'It is a medium figure, would you say?'

Bridge scowled. 'I am not a medium. I've exposed enough of those charlatans –'

James slammed his hand down: she jumped. 'Fire, I think,' he smiled, 'don't you? You drink, you smoke, you whore yourself out at times. A wild party. Drunk to excess. A dropped cigarette.' He shook his head. 'Such a tragic situation, isn't it Bridge? You are just beginning to get your life together, aren't you?'

'Do you want me to beg?' she asked quietly. If I can keep him talking long enough –

'Oh, Bridge. Bridge. Bridge. I had respect for you, d'you know? Brilliant. Troubled. No –' He grinned; leered. 'Tortured. A mass of problems but helping others with this –' he clicked his fingers. 'What do you call it?'

'Interactive grief counselling solutions.'

James snorted, shaking his head. 'You just talk to your clients? Or do you have to touch something of the deceased's?'

Bridge shook her head, shifting her feet in the heels. 'No. I act as a conduit. A bridge.'

She lunged at him across the desk. He went for something in his jacket pocket but too slow: she held his hand between hers.

It was eternal night overhead. The bridge was beneath her, was her, a grand, elaborate construct with balustrades and stanchions, gothic stonework and marble statues.

James was beside her. 'What the Holy Mary Mother of God –'

Bridge took a step away from him. The darkness seemed – thicker – around him. 'This is my world.' She smiled sadly. 'Out there, it's hard. But in here, there's just me. No addictions. No pain. No regret.'

There were wisps of colour, traces of pastel, closing in on their location from both sides of the bridge.

'In here,' she repeated, 'there is just myself and the spirits of the dead. They want to talk to you, James.' She took a step towards him.

James backed away. 'No. What? How –'

'Sandhra was the first, wasn't she, James? Your wife.' Bridge took another step towards him.

The pastel shades were taking on form and feature.

'Then Josephus. A quiet little accountant. Never hurt anyone except the taxman.' She grinned. 'Well James? Do you see them?'

He looked up. The blue was gone from his eyes. They were colourless.

'Nikoletta Smith. The last important person to you. They stopped being accidents after her. Tramps. Runaways. Drug users. How many did you prey on, James?'

Legion was forming around him, a wall of light around the darkness that engulfed him.

He shook his head, his eyes glinting silver in the darkness. 'I was warned, but I didn't believe him. It was too far-fetched.' He scowled. 'A dainty young thing. Easy prey, I thought. So easy. An accident, here or there. So helpful to the Police. You give a little, you can take a little, you know?'

He took a step towards her, the darkness holding back the light that called his name, that cried his name, that cursed his name.

'Do you —' she hesitated a moment; he was stronger than she'd expected. 'Do you regret them? Do you wish to atone?'

James sighed, a very mortal trait. 'It's too late for that, little girl.'

Bridge shivered. It was James' voice, but for a moment there, it had sounded just like her mentor —

'You know who has me; I cannot escape. I need to do this. It's nothing personal; I like you. I wish I'd known about your abilities before —'

Bridge closed her eyes. Concentrated. The bridge was underfoot, around, above.

She was sat at her desk still, holding James' hand. She released it.

The darkness broke and the bridge was gone and the headache exploded behind her eyes. Bridge clutched her head, tears of pain stinging her cheeks as she lost control of her bladder.

She forced her eyes open, the light and the tears making everything blurry. James stared at her, sightless, departed, stranded on the bridge, caught between life and death, nothing but a husk.

Pain rose from inside of her and she was dragged down, dragged into unconsciousness.

Falling to Apotheosis

Darkness. Darkness without end, without beginning: darkness infinite. A place outside time, without dimensions, inflexible and constant.

Traceries of light that could have burned in the Heavens for a century, or passed in the blink of an eye.

Flashes of colour – green, violet, gold, that burned bright, that burned radiant where no eye could see them.

The traceries of light led off the original spark. A deep crimson that burned the Heavens or the neural pathways with a flaming incandescence.

The colours, the traceries, spread, thickened, joined up, became a net to hold the sky in, to strain the spirit through, to catch the soul.

--

Pain and a body and a sense of dislocation and she was falling and she was suddenly human and screaming her pain with vocal cords that had not existed a moment before as her principle was ripped open and life thrust out of her womb and she was heavy and earth bound and the pain made her –

--

A hand mopped her brow. Darkness, but the darkness of shadows. Half shaded, a candle flame flickered. A warm, damp, towel on her forehead. The smell of wood smoke and incense. The sound of a voice talking, but the words meant nothing to her. A slight breeze, cool on her skin. A rug over her legs, warm and soft and furry.

The sudden strident cry of a child. Fresh and raw and powerful, seeming to come from all around her.

Movement. A disturbance in the half light. She could just make out the figure moving, lifting something. The sound distorted; changed.

A sudden weight on her chest. Clammy lips, a mouth, closing on her nipple.

Warmth. Movement. Milk flowing in her breast.

A second weight on her chest. A second mouth drawing sustenance from her.

Arms. Hands. Movement.

They were small her hands told her. Newborn; not old.

Children. Her children.

A son and daughter.

There was so much she knew. So much she didn't.

Time. It was all a matter of time.

--

Stars. The traceries had been stars.

Brilliant, extravagant displays of them, cascading across the Heavens.

Crimson, gold and turquoise, colliding and reforming. Firework displays and pyrotechnic illusions blazing behind her eyes.

Stars. Falling, or maybe ascending.

--

'And how are we doing today?'

A hand mopped her brow. Large, pale, callused. A man's hand, but gentle.

'Nirmila tells me the babies are doing well, so that's good. I'll tell you –' the speaker paused, replacing the dry towel on her head with a damp one, 'no one knows what to do with you. Sirdar thinks you're the goddess Lakshmi, or some such. Crops have done well. All the men have done well on their portering. No one has died. There's not been a year like it for a long time.'

A damp cloth mopped her cheeks and chin, her throat.

'I hope you don't think I'm trying anything but Sirdar thinks you're a goddess and Nirmila will only check on the children –' the man's voice trailed off.

It was a pleasant, relaxing, voice. The damp cloth ran down her arms, washing each finger. Her arms were lifted one after the other, the underarm washed. She heard the towel dropped in a bowl; squeezed, drips falling from it.

'We had to name the children. The locals were very determined on that point.'

The damp towel wiped one breast, then the other. The motion caused the lakes to curl and coil and milk spilled out.

'Your son is named Ahimsa.' The rug was lifted. The damp cloth passed over her belly and the rug lowered. 'Your daughter is named Karma. They are good Hindu names.'

The man chuckled. It was still shadowed: she couldn't see his face.

'Suresh Thapa, he is a good man, he thinks you should go to Kathmandu.'

He was cleaning the cloth again. Where he'd cleaned tingled.

She couldn't speak, she didn't know his name – she didn't know her own name – but his voice and gentle touch was a comfort. A lifeline. A link to humanity, to hold her when the stars called.

'I have sent messages to Kathmandu and all the villages nearby, to see who you are, but it is unusual.'

She could hear the smile in his voice.

'You are unusual. I am not sure you are a goddess, but the Nepalese are closer to their gods than I am, so perhaps you are.'

The rug settled on her legs. She hadn't even felt his touch for his voice, and now her legs tingled pleasantly.

'I will leave you now. Sleep well, my Lakshmi.'

She could hear him moving and see the shadows shifting.

A distant door opened –

and the press of bodies crowding the doorway and the maelstrom of faces peering at her, the smell of incense and shit, and a summer's day, brutal and cold, a high peaked mountain and a forest beyond the village and beyond all the chaos –

– and closed.

--

The web encircled her. A patchwork quilt of stars, parcelling the darkness out between them and the darkness was beautiful but not as beautiful as the stars. Emerald. Lilac. Jasmine. The lines got thinner and thinner, the traceries finer, until there was no darkness in her perspective, only the colours diminishing and diminishing.

But the colours were there. The traceries. The stars.

Surrounding her. Protecting her. Loving her in their cold, brittle, brilliant, distant way.

--

'I do not know if this is doing any good. If you can hear me. But I will go on speaking to you until you tell me otherwise.'

The dry cloth was removed from her forehead. The backs of his fingers stroked her brow. His touch made her tingle: raised sweat on her skin; caused a prickling sensation.

His fingers traced down one cheek to her chin.

'I – do not mean to be inappropriate,' he said slowly, 'but touch may be as important as sound.' His fingers slipped across her lips gently.

'Sirdar has forbidden Suresh from taking you to Kathmandu.' He gave a snort of laughter. 'Suresh has forbidden Sirdar from letting the villagers worship you.'

She heard him drag a chair over. For a moment his breath was warm on her arm.

'So that leaves you and me, Lakshmi.' He chuckled, and she tried to imagine the smile illuminating the face she'd never seen. 'And Ahimsa and Karma, though Nirmila looks after them except when they are hungry.'

She heard movement, heard water, and then he laid a damp cloth on her forehead again.

'Everyone's talking about you.' His voice seemed distant: from further away, though he hadn't appeared to move. 'You're the talk of the Himalayas.' He sighed.

She wanted to reach out to him, to take his hand, but there was dislocation and she was only an echo and he was only a voice and it was perfect like that and to touch would spoil the moment.

'I don't suppose you remember what happened? Would you tell me if you could?' he had moved: his breath was warm on her shoulder.

'They found you not far from the village. I don't know if it was a coma or deep unconsciousness, but nothing could wake you.'

He chuckled again, low and deep. It tightened something deep within her. It caused an ache, a yearning.

'Nothing that is, until Karma decided she wanted to be born. Where she opened the way, Ahimsa followed.'

--

Stars twinkled. They weren't stars but eyes, winking at her.

The eyes of her children. The eyes of the stars.

The colours were all around her. She was part of the colour, part of the net, part of the circumference of the Heavens. She burned fire gold and purple jade; lilac, saffron and damask.

--

'I must leave you now, but I will find you again, Lakshmi. I will find you and we will have the darkness and the stars.'

He bent over her. His breath blossomed across her face. His lips brushed her forehead and her eyes. He kissed her lips and the stars became traceries of light in her body, in her blood and in her milk.

She couldn't contain the pleasure that exploded from his touch and she became the darkness, investing the stars with her powers and she became the stars, illuminating the darkness with her presence. She became the universe, unravelling and recoiling. She became the realities, branching apart from each other and seamlessly blending in to one.

She came to herself in the sun-dried mud hut, the rug around her knees, drenched in sweat and sated.

She placed a hand on her belly and sat up. The door opened and Nirmila came in, carrying her babies. She scooted back until she could lean on the wall and took her children off the little Sherpa woman. The woman tucked the rug up over her hips again.

'Suresh is going to ask if anyone knows who you are.' The woman studied her face. 'You're not China. Or Mongol. India, perhaps? But so tall.' She shook her head. 'I will have to make clothes to fit you. No man must see you like this.' She patted Lakshmi's hand absently. 'It is not spoken about. It is private.'

Nirmila grinned suddenly. 'Not that there is any suitable man for a day's walk on any path from here. But you are not Sherpa girl. Not Gurung either. Make good wife, but you have children already. No family.' She shrugged. 'No dowry.'

She closed her eyes. She was warm and tired and spent. There was so much she knew and so much she didn't. If the stars knew they weren't saying.

Time. It was all a matter of time.

Love As A Gene Code

She spotted him before he'd got halfway across Market Place. He wore jeans and a sweatshirt and walked fast, standing out from the locals. A figure ran ahead of him, bobbing and weaving, constantly beckoning to him, drawing him on, away from the doorway, away from his entrance to her world.

Amaranthaceae quickened her pace. She didn't know how he'd found a guide so quickly or why he wasn't staring around in wonderment, but those questions were irrelevant. He was an Incomer. An alien. A threat. She dealt with threats daily, quickly, quietly, without any qualms.

His guide was leading him across the Broad Way, a cobbled way worn smooth by cart wheels and camel hooves. Down his guide led him, towards the Oracle.

It was then she hastened. The Oracle was to be protected. The doorway was in too public a place to block or to watch, but the slow trickle of strangers had not been unnoticed: she'd heard traders talking about it. The Oracle would know what to do. She'd arrest the Incomer then seek the Oracle's advice.

The guide left the road and entered the Oracle's field. It was muddy, close to the Kennet, and brightly coloured tents adorned it. The locals eyed her curiously, a few disappearing into their tents as she gripped the hilt of her sword. The guide was leading the Incomer straight towards the Oracle.

A figure moved to stop her and without breaking stride she pushed and tripped him, leaving him sprawling in the mud. The guide was almost at the Oracle's tent. Though two Irregulars guarded it, they could have been bought off.

Two more figures interposed themselves.

'Captain, this is not –'

She left the speaker gasping for breath, the second flat on his back. The tent flap was being held open by the Irregulars and the guide was gesturing the Incomer to step inside.

Amaranthaceae stared.

'Mohan? Mohan, what –'

The tent flaps closed on the Oracle's serving boy and the Incomer. She strode forwards, the two Irregulars staring at her nervously.

'Captain, the Oracle –'

She punched the speaker out, sending him flying. The second shuffled about, uneasy.

'We had our orders, captain. The Oracle –'

Amaranthaceae lifted the Irregular by his djellaba so he was face to face with her.

'Were you a Janissary, you would be heading for the block now,' she hissed. 'You do not let an Incomer in to see the Oracle.'

The Oracle was highly regarded by the Committee, but separate from both the Hashishim and the Janissaries. Only the Irregulars, low grade responsible citizens, were allowed to defend her. Maybe this is Wizerbowski's plan: he is grooming Mohan to join the Hashishim when he is of age. Wizerbowski is no more happy about leaving the Oracle protected by Irregulars than I am. If this is his plan to force more capable guards upon her –

All this passed through her mind in an instant.

She thrust the tent flaps aside, drawing her sword and entering.

A dozen lamps cast diffuse, pale golden light. The Incomer sat cross legged, innocently sipping tea. Mohan sat in the corner, the silver teapot and cups before him as usual and a bowl of sweet pastries. The Oracle –

'Captain Ramzy, you are out of order.' The Oracle was standing, her pale eyes narrowed. 'You were taught to show respect to the Oracles, were you not? You do not simply barge in, sword drawn.'

Amaranthaceae stared for a moment, then lowered her gaze, fumbling to sheathe her sword. 'My apologies, Oracle. I was following the Incomer –'

'Guards.'

Two Irregulars stepped into the tent.

'Escort the captain from my presence. See to it that she is given twenty lashes for her insolence, then bring her back to me.'

Amaranthaceae stared. 'Oracle –'

The Oracle sat down. The Irregulars took her by the arms and led her away.

--

Amaranthaceae could still taste the blood and salt and sweat in her mouth from the gag. The Irregulars lowered her down and she was able to cross her legs. Her weapons belt had been removed prior to the flogging, along with all her weapons. Her back was heavy, tight, painful. Her under tunic clung to the fresh weals and every movement hurt.

'Do you know why I had that done to you?'

She looked up. The Oracle was sitting, almost demurely, sipping at her mint tea. Mohan had already placed a cup in front of her, keeping his gaze averted, but she had no inclination to touch it.

'You are wild, captain, an untamed beast.' The Oracle shook her head. 'This is a civilised town. We are far from being a frontier. You handle your duties well, with tact and discretion. But that does not give you the right to enter my tent with a drawn sword.'

Amaranthaceae drew the cup closer but didn't drink.

'I would suggest you have the tea. Its sweetness will ease the pain, I am sure.'

Still she didn't drink.

'Was it humiliating?'

She raised her head. 'I was stripped to the waist and publicly flogged.' She fought to control her voice. 'By Irregulars.'

The Oracle shook her head. 'No. Your jerkin and over tunic were removed. You held your under tunic to your chest. I would not have a woman stripped publicly.' She smiled. 'Was the humiliation the flogging, or the fact it was done by Irregulars?'

Amaranthaceae looked away. They'd given her a gag to bite down on but not chained or bound her in any way. Plenty of the folk of the Oracle had watched her shame as the pain had made her clench her hands tighter and tighter, struggling not to fight back, not to defend herself, not to simply punch out the Irregular carrying out the punishment.

'Would you rather I had requested punishment through channels? You are the Janissary officer responsible for this town, but the Committee gives orders to the Hashishim.'

She looked down at the ground. Her back burned. Her front ached.

'Their punishment would have been on record. You are too useful a tool to be damaged that way.'

'Damaged?' Amaranthaceae looked up.

The Oracle took a sip of her tea. 'Do you know how rare you are, Amaranthaceae? A female captain of the Janissaries. Such a thing would be unheard of in Jerusalem or Jordan. You have done well; achieved much.'

She took a sip of the tea. It had been an honour, being sent to Reading. The responsibility of defending the world against Incomers was hers. The responsibility of protecting the Oracle was unofficially hers. But –

'It is time you remembered you are female and acted accordingly.'

Amaranthaceae raised her gaze. 'What?'

The Oracle smiled. 'I have found your perfect partner. The Incomer. His name is Gabriel.'

She stared at the Oracle. 'What?'

'You are on a dangerous road, Amaranthaceae. You need not tread it alone. Gabriel is perfect for you.'

Amaranthaceae shook her head. 'I don't need anyone. I am proud of my job. I am good at it. I don't need,' she repeated.

'But what about children?'

She stared, feeling herself blush slightly. 'What about children?'

The Oracle's smile broadened. 'You cannot have children without a husband. I have found the perfect match for you. More than ideal, he is your genetically compatible life mate.'

Amaranthaceae shook her head again. 'I have no interest in acquiring a husband. I love my job. I do not need –'

'I have gone to considerably effort and expenditure to track him down.'

Amaranthaceae scowled, crossing her arms and wincing; lowered them. 'I suppose if I say no you'll have me flayed again.'

The Oracle sighed. 'Grow up, Amaranthaceae. Who have you really got that is just for you? Gabriel will support you, temper you, make you a better officer –'

'You think I'm not a good officer?'

'I think you're an exceedingly good officer.'

Amaranthaceae stared. Blinked.

'I know the code of the Janissaries and the Hashishim. To marry one of them is every woman's dream. But for a man to marry you? You intimidate them. Your position. Your personality. Your strength. So I have had to look – elsewhere.'

'An Incomer?'

The Oracle nodded. 'Gabriel waits for you outside. Talk to him. Do not say no. Just —' she paused, sighing. 'Just consider it. Please, Amaranthaceae.'

--

'I am sorry.'

Amaranthaceae looked at the Incomer. He had mousy brown hair. Was shorter than her. She frowned.

'I mean, this is all —' he waved his hand, 'but you were doing your job and got flogged for it.' He frowned. 'Is it a normal punishment? It seems pretty crude.'

She held out her hand. An Irregular came scurrying over, laden with her sword belt and weapons. As she took them he ran off again, trying to keep his face hidden.

'I mean, what do I know of your world? I didn't believe it at first. When Mohan explained to me what was going on. I mean – a bookshop opening into other realities. Come on, I thought. But then he mentioned you, said we'd be right together.'

She tightened the belt, gritting her teeth and trying not to wince as the jacket pulled across her back.

'Does it hurt?'

Amaranthaceae walked away.

--

It was night before she left the apartment. She'd stripped until she wore only her under tunic, letting the water from the shower soak it before she edged it away from her back. Some of the scabs had broken, bleeding, but the pain was second hand, distant, removed. Her front was bruised, the marks where her fingers had dug into her breasts clear.

What would it be like with a man she'd wondered, as she'd washed her hair. Would he be gentle or would it hurt. Would it hurt more than being flogged or less. She'd touched the bruises tenderly. Would he kiss them better, she wondered –

Amaranthaceae pulled her hand away. No man could alleviate pain. That wasn't the problem. The problem, as far as she was concerned, was the Oracle.

She found what she was looking for on the third attempt. If she'd gone in uniform she'd have had no chance, but she was able to slip in and talk to him, cajole him, reassure him, until he told her what she needed to know.

'Thank you,' she whispered, slipping out of his tent.

'Well, what do we have here?'

In the moonlight she could see six men clearly. A couple carried clubs; two had staves. Two appeared to be unarmed.

'This is out of bounds at night, woman.'

The leader of the gang stepped closer, the others forming a loose semicircle and closing around her.

'Women only come here at night for one thing, and you wouldn't have got it from that tent.'

'You don't want to do this.'

The speaker sniggered. 'I do. I really do. Hold her.'

Two of the thugs closed in on either side. She let them get near then spun and kicked one; grabbed the other as he tried to catch her and pulled him off balance.

The other four closed in. She dropped to her knees and kicked out, tripping one. As she rose another ploughed into her, bringing her down. She cried out as pain exploded across her back.

Amaranthaceae lashed out but a meaty hand grabbed her wrist. A weight was across her legs and her other arm was caught: she was pinned.

'Hey. She's still got the bracelet. Oh, by Allah and Christ we've got ourselves a real prize – a feisty virgin.'

Another sniggered. 'No wonder she was in the wrong tent.'

Hands gripped her shoulders: she was pulled up. Hands like paws groped her chest. Amaranthaceae bit her lip.

'She can't be.' Her blouse was ripped open: clammy hands thrust inside her under tunic.

She fought not to shudder as hands fondled her breasts.

'What man wouldn't want these?'

'Leave her,' the leader snapped. 'Let me see her face.'

Her head was yanked back. Fingers gripped her chin.

'She took down two of us,' the guy on her back moaned, 'we're entitled to a little –'

'No. I need to think about this.'

'What's to think about? The four of us owe her. She's on her own –'

The guy on her back moved off, hand on her hip to roll her. She let him, then kicked him in the crotch, slamming her knee into his head as he collapsed.

The blade of a knife touched her throat. 'That wasn't very nice, but it was understandable. Just so you don't get any more ideas –'

Pain exploded in her stomach as the club landed and she screamed, twisting. Her blouse and under tunic tore away –

'She's been flogged.'

'Who'd flog a virgin?'

'I should hold it there, gentlemen.'

Amaranthaceae looked up, tears of pain in her eyes, as she heard Wizerbowski's voice. The Hashishim officer carried an odd looking pair of weapons, somewhere between blow guns and crossbows.

'Who're you?' the leader demanded.

'And what are those?'

There was a faint puff of sound. One of the thugs collapsed.

'He's dead, I assure you. I suggest you let the lady go.'

'Now see here,' the leader began.

Amaranthaceae grabbed his hand as Wizerbowski fired, forcing the knife away from her neck as he collapsed behind her. The remaining thug broke and ran.

Amaranthaceae sat up slowly. She could feel the blood trickling down her back once more, and down her neck where the blade had scratched her.

'The Oracle's quarter is a dangerous place after dark, Amar. You know that.'

She nodded. 'I had to. There's something more dangerous than the Oracle's quarter at night. But how did you find me?'

Wizerbowski grinned. 'Gabriel. The Oracle told him to stay with you, that you were worth the effort.' His weapons disappeared. 'So what's more dangerous than here at night, and don't say you.'

--

He found her a tunic and wanted her to wait 'til morning, but Amaranthaceae only waited until he'd confirmed what she needed to know. She silenced the dozing Irregulars and stepped into the Oracle's tent.

'I'm a light sleeper, you know.'

The Oracle had large glasses on and her hair looked uncombed. Mohan was not in the corner – none of her runners were, of course, and the absence seemed momentarily strange.

'Good. I've figured it out. You've been using the doorway. Sending Mohan or others through. Do the Committee know?'

The Oracle scowled, but Amaranthaceae saw the momentary fear. 'Don't presume to lecture me, girl. When you've born three children –'

'Yes, Sibyl, I'm glad you reminded me. Gabriel is staying. He's my evidence, you see, that you've been tinkering in other realities. The Committee want the door watched; they don't want it forced open.'

The Oracle snorted. 'Since when do you know what the Committee want? You are only a lonely Janissary off –'

'Since Wizerbowski contacted his superiors.' She smiled sweetly. 'They confirmed death to all Incomers and any assisting them.'

'But Mohan was the one –'

'Yes.' She nodded. 'I spoke to Mohan this morning. I think, in the interests of his safety, that he will stay with me from now on.'

The Oracle snorted. 'He's no use to you. He can't,' she stopped, the realisation on her face.

'I know what you did to him.' Amaranthaceae took a half step closer to her. 'Wizerbowski is fetching Mohan's papers. I'm taking legal guardianship of him.'

'You know nothing about raising a child –'

Amaranthaceae shrugged. 'I can't do worse than you. Suppressing the child's hormones. Tinkering with the fate of all realities for your own ends.' She shrugged. 'I'll be taking Mohan far away from this place – the doorway corrupts.'

She smiled. 'But don't worry about Gabriel. Wizerbowski has found a place for him in the Hashishim. They'll be keeping an eye on the doorway. And you.'

The Oracle stared at her, fuming. 'You can't do this.'

Amaranthaceae shrugged. It was spoiled by the wince as a scab pulled but she grinned anyway. 'I can do it through channels if you prefer. But when the Committee find out –'

She shook her head. 'You're good for the public. Be good for the public, and pray nothing happens to Mohan, Gabriel, Wizerbowski or myself, because if it anything does –'

Amaranthaceae walked off into the night and her new life to collect her adopted son.

Falling from the moon

Shimmering, incandescent blue. Sunlight reflecting, bold stabs of gold and yellow piercing her shroud. Twinkling, sparkling, calling to her. A single step, a dive, and it would be over. Release. An end of the pain. Surrender. An end to the hurt and confusion.

Surrender, the waves called to her, lapping against the buttresses of the bridge. The wind tore her hair and the salt spray stung her eyes, made her nose twitch.

Sound was almost gone. There was no one on the walkway in either direction. The occasional rumble, as of distant thunder, as a car roared past, fast and dangerous, death traps of metal and gas.

Louise gripped the rail of the bridge, fingers going numb despite the fingerless gloves. The wind pulled at her coat, wrapped cold hands around her in horrifying personal ways. She wanted to tug the coat closed but was afraid to relinquish the rail. Only the rail was real. Only the rail kept her safe.

Her teeth chattered. The water was beautiful but it was cold as well, cold and icy, like diamonds. Diamonds. She shivered. Like the diamond on her mother's engagement ring. Twinkling cold, leering bold, like Col, the giver – Louise flinched, tearing one hand from the rail. Cars roared past, oblivious.

One bound. The right time. A fast car. Too fast, too late to stop – she felt sick and turned away. Squeamish. It would hurt. She didn't want it to hurt. Enough had hurt already.

Groping hands. She'd brought her boot down on one. Been back handed; slapped in the face. The bruise had dulled to blue with the promise of more. She'd flinched. Backed away. Hands, everywhere.

The water serenaded her. It wasn't cold. It was warm. It loved her. It would take her away from all pain, all memory, all grief. Join me, the water called. Join me. Slip away to the river.

I'll take you out to the sea. Far from prying hands. Far from the hurt. Join me. The sea called her. The sea is forever. Nothing can hurt us again.

A gull screeched overhead, backwinging against the wind, caught, trapped, unable to progress. It cried again, and Louise shut her eyes.

Crying was wrong. Crying was a clue that something was wrong. Nothing was wrong so she mustn't cry. Mustn't spoil her mother's happiness.

The gull cried again and Louise felt the tears sting her eyes. The gull twisted in midair. Was borne away without another cry.

The salt wind scoured her cheeks. Breathed into her neck, making her shiver. Slipped between the tails of her coat, touching her legs. She trembled. Almost fell. Tightened the grip on the safety rail. It was the only real thing. It was the only safety, the only sanctuary.

She'd told her mother. The woman who had been her mother, once. Col had poisoned her mother's mind, twisted the words she said until they were ash in her mouth. She'd been grounded. He'd gloated.

Something soared past her, a can, thrown from a car, caught by the wind. Thrown at her, the stupid Goth girl, crying all alone where no one would see her. No one would talk to her. She'd stopped talking a long time ago. No one listened. No one believed.

The wind dropped and the clouds parted. The sun, wanting to get next to her, wanting her to open her clothes to him. She spared one hand from the rail to clutch the sweater to her neck. Not again. Never again.

Col's face in the darkness was always there. His hands, like a ghost, his fingers cold, touching, prying –

Louise squirmed. The rail would protect her. If he came – if anyone came –. The river waited for her. The river was patient. The river would take her away from everyone. The river understood.

It had been no better, away from him. Desperate and always cold, lonely, afraid, selling what little she had to survive. Anything was better than him.

A car roared by; someone jeered from the window. The little Goth girl, like a frozen, wind-lashed statue. The church had offered no sanctuary, the Laundromat only warmth. Warmth that made her hungry and that drove her back to the street.

The wind was rising. She'd buttoned the jacket but it was warmer wrapped around. The elbows were threadbare. The front was stained, torn. Cold steel buttons from half forgotten, unremembered bands filled the collars. Nicholas' jacket. His buttons. It was the only thing he'd had, the only thing she'd saved from the squat.

Louise dug her fingers into a pocket. Wrappers, the cigarettes long since smoked. A bent spoon. Silver foil. Tuppence. The top of a bottle. She threw them to the waiting river below. She smelled, for a moment, the smoke and fire, the nicotine, the alcohol, the smell of burning –

Louise flinched. She'd barely got out alive. She touched her hair with nervous fingers. The right side was shorn, shrivelled from the fire. She'd staggered, beating at the heat. Nicholas had liked to stroke her hair, to run his fingers through its luxurious growth. That was reason enough not to miss it. She'd cut the rest short as soon as she'd been able to steal a pair of scissors.

A gull appeared, circling overhead. Her stepfather Col. Her mother. The man she'd run to, Nicholas, who'd taken what she had and taught her to steal, hooked her, punched her. Its cries distracted her. He'd screeched like that, at the height of his pleasure. She'd shut her mind away then. Been a china doll.

Porcelain features. A painted expression, fragile and hard. The gull slammed into the wires, its wings entangled. It gave a hideous, pitiful squawk. Sheared away, white feathers fluttering down.

The feathers whipped around, wind tossed, storm lost, scattered. If she went home; if he found her. If she went to the squat; if the Police found her. If she left here, the sea would never find her.

The silver foil glittered like a crown around a feather. Another feather was entangled with a piece of plastic, the webbing from a six pack. Caught, with nowhere to go. Caught and borne out to the waiting arms of the sea.

A car squealed behind her, changing gears, roaring on. There was movement in the distance. She half turned. Someone was on the walkway, approaching her, but still a distance away.

The water called to her. It would be gentle. It loved her. All she had to do was cross the rail. The rail was no longer protecting her. It was preventing her.

A car slowed. Stopped. Voices. Raised voices.

There was no protection anywhere. No safety. No sanctuary. Col had found her. He would take her back again. He would make her suffer in silence until he was sated.

Louise cringed, tearing her hands from the rail. The rail leered at her. It stopped her. It had been on his side all along, slowing her, delaying her, until he could be fetched.

I cannot fight him. All my pain and anger; I cannot stop him.

She took a step forwards.

An authoritarian voice told her to stop. Told her to step away from the rail.

The rail betrayed me. I don't want to touch it –

Just for an instant. A moment's action. Join us, the water whispered. The rail is all that holds you back. We will take you to safety. Back to your childhood. Back to warmth and security.

Louise. Col's voice, breaking, trying to be gentle.

Louise dear. A woman's voice. The woman who had once been her mother. Who had betrayed her.

A gull flew by overhead, winging its way out to sea. The waves whispered, the water welcomed her.

We know you didn't mean it. The authoritarian voice. We know you're not to blame for the fire. We've contacted Social Services. They can help –

The clouds cleared. Sunlight broke through the waves. Golden shimmering and blue incandescent. Silver and white, turquoise and lavender.

The rail was cold beneath her fingers and then the wind lifted her, taking her to the river, the river taking her out to sea.

The Bookshop My Mistress

Rob unplugged the earphones and switched the Blackberry off automatically. He was theoretically on call 24/7 but the Bookshop was his sanctuary. Work had been building up for the past few years, and since Cal – he'd buried himself in his work. Six to nine wasn't an unusual working day, doing almost as much in two days as most did in five. And then doing three more days. And occasionally weekends. There was no reason not to; all the reason to.

He pushed the door open. The Bookshop smelt of dust, and that peculiar scent – a combination of floor polish, air freshener and thousands of pages of aged, printed text – which libraries often exhibited.

He knew it was archaic. Technically obsolete. Anything he needed he could find online. There wasn't room in the house in Mill Gardens for anything more than half a dozen slim volumes. Nothing but the latest Booker prize winners or chat show celebrity volumes intended to show to your dinner party guests how rounded an individual – a couple – you were.

But a deeper part of him, something raw which Cal's absence had exposed, needed them. The door shut behind him, taking with it the traffic and the demands of work and entering him into a little haven of peace. Something melodic and faintly classical was playing on the stereo – stereo he thought, his hardened love of new technology rising for a moment.

The woman at the till looked up and smiled and he smiled back and his calm tranquillity returned. The Bookshop was a success. Now books were unnecessary – just as CDs were unnecessary because they could be downloaded – they had become more popular than ever before.

He recognised the woman as the manageress. If 'The Bookshop' had taken after her, then she must be out of step with society, faintly unworldly, a shelter against the storm of life. She was tall and thin, older than him, with sparkling blue eyes. He knew it was a cliché but her smile – her eyes – did transform her face. It transformed her from a scarecrow to he didn't know what. The last bastion of Englishness, of calm politeness, of an old fashioned world that had all but been eroded elsewhere. The archetypal English rose he thought, a woman who in another era would do coffee mornings and make cucumber sandwiches; further back, would man – person, surely – the barricades and then join the Women's Institute.

He passed by a table display, idly curious, not particularly looking for anything specific. That was another reason for liking the shop. It was quirky and experimental and flawed in a way the chain bookshops weren't. It was also, he realised, wholly human, in a world gone technologically supernova.

'Was there anything you were looking for?'

Rob looked up at the woman, aware he'd picked a book up, aware that she had the faintest trace of an accent, though he couldn't tell where it was from.

'No. I,' he looked at the book he'd picked up. A lay person's guide to the Gnostic Chronicles. He smiled, shook his head and replaced it on the table.

There were posters on display, but not film, reality TV or boy band tie-in. There were reproductions of WWII adverts and tasteful Indian prints and Old Masters.

He turned back to the till. 'No. I was just –' he didn't know what he was just.

'You just wanted to spend some time.'

Something she'd said brought a smile to Rob's face. He nodded. 'I didn't want to rush home. Not tonight. It's my – it was our – anniversary. The house isn't cold but it is empty without Cal –' he shrugged, uncertain why he was telling her, a virtual stranger.

'How long has it been?'

'Three years.' She understood. 'Cal walked out on me.' She'd been through something similar. 'Police found her body two days later.' There was something tender and kind about her that he'd not seen in anyone else. Not that he'd been looking. 'Suicide. I don't know why.'

'I can stay open late tonight. If you want to browse. I can even run to a cup of coffee, if you like.'

Rob chuckled, feeling like he'd admitted to a childhood crush and shook his head. 'No. I'm sure you've got a home to go to. Children that need feeding. Or grandkids to babysit. I should –'

Her expression froze. For an instant he thought he saw uncertainty and confusion and anger in her gaze but then it was locked down.

'I –'

In the pause he could have repainted the shop.

' – always wanted children. My husband said he did but he wasn't capable. And now –' she sighed and her expression cracked. The anger was gone, leaving only uncertainty and confusion.

' – now I find he's lied his whole life.'

'Another woman?'

She shook her head. 'That I might understand. But this – ' she shook her head again, her mask in place once more. 'Never mind. It's gone closing time. I'll be open tomorrow and the weekend as normal, if you want to browse.'

She half smiled. 'I don't suppose you want to work here or know anyone who might?'

He shook his head.

'There always seems to be different staff. You must have a lot of –'

She shrugged. 'Turnover's high. One's gone ill. Two more moved away. But –'

Rob nodded. 'I'll browse another day. If I think of anyone, I'll let you know.'

--

Her smile saw him home. He'd bottled it up. Known he'd bottled it up. But it'd been perfect with Cal. Known her for nearly twenty years. Married for a dozen years. They'd been talking about kids. He was earning enough for the both of them – for all of them. She could return to her job in a couple of years; he'd go part time then. They had all the plans worked out.

There hadn't been an argument, not a falling out or a tiff. She'd simply gone out to the shops – and drowned in the Thames.

Maybe it is time, he thought. Cut back on the hours. Spend more time – browsing. A smile lingered on his lips. Find that special someone, the old-fashioned way –

He unlocked the front door and pushed it open and knew instantly someone was there.

He could smell the chilli and the rich aroma of venison the same moment he heard the singing. It had been his favourite dish – Cal's speciality – venison with chilli and chocolate. She cooked like an angel and sung like a chef.

He ran through the sitting room, hearing the kitchen door open.

'I've called the Police. I'm not afraid –'

Rob slid to a halt, staring at the impossible. Cal stood in the kitchen doorway, holding a rolling pin in her hand.

'Rob?'

'Cal?'

She was in his arms again, impossible, alive, warm, kissing him –

He pushed her away angrily.

'You're dead. I saw you.' He sunk his nails into his palms. 'I identified your body. It was –' he shuddered.

Cal was staring, shaking her head. 'It was you. Three years ago. A policeman and woman called. I was worried. You'd just gone out for some milk. There I was hoping you'd just –' she looked away, shaking her head. 'You're dead, Rob. I'm just –' she sighed. 'Drunk or dreaming. This isn't real.'

Cal was so real. She wore the terrible jumper his mother had given her. A towel round her waist and her hair wrapped in another.

She was too much. He pulled her into his arms, kissing her, pulling the towel from her hair. Her hair spilled across her shoulders, just as he remembered it.

'Rob.' She pushed him away. 'It's been three years. Why did you do it? Why fake your death? Was living with me so terrible?'

He drew her back into his embrace, loosening the towel from her hips.

'Cal. Three years ago you walked out on me. The police –' he broke off, remembering the naked body they'd fished from the Thames. The woman had drowned. Cal had drowned. Even if he hadn't recognised her, her dental records and fingerprints correlated. It was savage, looking at her lying on the trolley like a slab of meat. Dead and naked and beautiful but dead, empty, vacant, departed, shuffled off the mortal coil, no more to be his sun and moon, his stars, his sky and his earth.

'Rob.' She caught at the towel and re-knotted it. 'We had a funeral for you. Your mother blamed me.' She paused. 'I'm sorry. Your father died not long after.'

He nodded, clinging to recognisable facts to steer through the surging white water threatening to capsize his sanity. 'I know. May tenth. His heart.'

Cal frowned. 'So you kept track but couldn't be bothered to come see me. Why, Rob? Why go all Reggie Perrin? Why come back now?'

Rob shook his head. 'I haven't been anywhere. This is my house. My –'

There was a photo of them, on their wedding day on the mantelpiece. A youthful photo of him. A photo of Cal, older, almost as she was before him, with an unknown man.

'Cal?' He looked around. There were plants in pots and the walls had been repainted a softer, pastel blue, something he'd always meant to do but never got round to.

'Rob?' she asked softly. 'Are you saying the past three years were – what? Fake? A test? Am I going mad?'

There was something in her gaze he'd never seen before. An unhinged aspect. She had been the most down to earth. His death – how can I have died – had obviously changed her, pushed her close to the edge.

'Rob?'

Her death pushed me into work. The chance to change that –

'Am I,' she shook her head. 'Do I need – do we need – to check into the Prospect Park Sanatorium, or is this all – did you – ' she fought against the sobs. 'What happened Rob?'

Rob drew her back into his arms and kissed her forehead. 'I'm sorry.'

I'm sorry Cal when you died I threw myself into work and I don't know what happened. Maybe you lost your memory. But I buried you. I had nothing to live for, for three years. I just existed. But I'd give it all up to be with you again, even if I daren't tell you the truth. I'd rather have you think me a louse than think yourself deluded. But when I look at you, I'll still see you as they pulled you from the Thames, and that's my punishment for lying to you.

70

'If you serve up, I'll tell you what I've been doing for the last three years.'

Cal smiled briefly, kissing his lips. 'It's ready. But, she paused.

'What?'

She shook her head. 'It doesn't matter.' Took his hand. 'Come on.'

Jacaranda's Volition

An electrifying, crackling, sound made her pause. In that instant there was a scream, rising high above the crowd of murmurs.

Feeling her heart lurch, Jacaranda hurried to the forum, jostling with the locals, using her height and her elbows to forge a path through.

Before the grand forum – which to her had always been the rundown Butts Centre – a man was being flogged. His back was a mass of bleeding weals. She swallowed her revulsion. The crowd seemed unconcerned; seemed to enjoy the spectacle.

A broad shouldered warrior, dressed in a skirt of leather strips and a padded leather cuirass, stepped forwards. He held a flagrum in his hand. She had time to notice he wore sandals and thick woollen socks, and then the man screamed again as the whip tore more skin from his back.

'Stop. Stop this. It is inhumane.'

Jacaranda pushed through the crowd. The warrior with the whip turned to face her. He ran his gaze up and down dismissively, then gazed at her again, slowly. She squirmed. His gaze made her feel like she was in the wrong.

'Legionnaire Caecilius is receiving punishment for a crime he committed. Do you know the punishment for interfering with the justice of the Roman Empire?'

She shook her head, belatedly aware there were more legionnaires in the crowd, closing in on her.

The Roman warrior gave her another long, slow look.

It would be comical, she thought, if it didn't feel real. I was in the bookshop. Henghist said no harm would befall me –

'By your appearance you are a druid. There is a standing warrant for any found to be taken before the nearest authority.' He grinned, leering. 'That would be Commander Valconius. It's been a while since we've watched a druid dance in the fire.'

73

He turned away, gave the legionnaire another, almost dismissive, lash. The man was bound to a pole, his arms stretched crosswise. His head had fallen and he gave no cry though she flinched.

'You cannot –'

Someone caught her arm – a legionnaire. Jacaranda pulled away violently. This is no longer – she stumbled, and arms clamped around her waist, pining her arms to her side. She slammed her head back and heard a crack: she was released, and someone was screaming, cursing her.

Jacaranda turned. If I can get back to the bookshop –

An arm swung her round. Pain exploded in her belly and she gagged, doubling over. Someone kicked her leg and she fell, face down on the cobbles. There was a heavy weight on her back and a hand seized her hair.

'Druids are trouble. One wrench and I'll break your neck. I'd rather not: I'll be in trouble with Valconius, but I'll do it if I must. Do you understand, druid?'

There was blood in her mouth. She spat. Licked her lips.

'Try anything,' the voice warned.

The point of a sword touched her neck. She couldn't nod. 'I promise.' Oh, Henghist why did I – she scowled. I wanted to. It was my choice.

The weight eased on her back, the sword sheathed. Her arms were pulled together and bound. She winced at the tightness.

'If you'd prefer, I could simply flog you here and now, then take you to the commander.'

Jacaranda was rolled onto her back. The broad shouldered warrior knelt beside her, one hand on the flagrum. She shook her head. 'No. I'll cooperate. Who are you?'

The warrior grinned, tucking his hands beneath her arms and lifting her to her feet. 'Quaestor Helvellyn. Can I just say it'll be a pleasure carrying out the punishment. Killing a druid is always an honour.'

'I'm not – you're – ' she frowned. 'You're Welsh.'

Helvellyn snorted. 'We've been part of the Empire for fifteen hundred years. We held out longer than the English. The Empire respected that. They don't respect terrorists.'

Jacaranda shook her head. 'I'm not a –'

His blow sent her staggering. Legionnaires caught her, held her, as the quaestor advanced on her once more. 'This is not a trial. Druids do not get trials. Commander Valconius will verify the death order. Then you will die. Or you will speak again and you will die and I will take your corpse to the commander. We can display your body either way.'

She closed her mouth tightly, glaring at Helvellyn. Henghist. You said I would be safe. You said nothing would harm me. She sighed as the cohort formed around her, as a pilum prodded her into movement.

Jacaranda stumbled on. They headed north, away from the forum. Scraps of mud and garbage hit her: the crowd was muttering angrily in her direction. The sun beat down and she could feel the blood on her cheeks, her lips. She felt woozy but gritted her teeth.

She didn't recognise the area she was passing through. If it was another Reading that Henghist had tempted her with, it was radically different.

Weren't the Romans defeated in three hundred, four hundred AD? My history isn't up to it. But in this reality, they survived. Flourished. She shook her head but it hurt. One of her teeth felt loose. I wouldn't believe it if I couldn't smell it.

They reached a low hill that curved up to the east and an impressive house. Station Hill, she thought. The station was on the brow. We're not far from where the shop is. Was. If I can escape –

There were a pair of soldiers guarding the be-pillared entrance to the house. Unlike the cohort and Helvellyn, who wore long red cloaks, these wore black cloaks.

The quaestor saw her look and grinned. 'The XIX. Caesar's elite originally. They were nothing until they were decimated. Discipline works wonders.' His grin faded. 'Except on troublesome druids. How many of your cult will you name before you die, I wonder?'

The cohort stopped before the entrance; wheeled away. The black cloaked soldiers came down. One stopped, sword drawn, at the base of the steps. Helvellyn backed away while the other approached her.

'Quaestor Helvellyn. I apprehended this druid at the forum, attempting to interfere with justice.'

The black cloaked soldier said nothing. Her arms were jerked. She only kept from crying out by biting her lips. Blood trickled from her mouth. The soldier frisked her professionally, without deference to her sex.

The door to the house opened. Two more black cloaked warriors descended, while the original two and Helvellyn escorted her up and in. She tried to turn her head as the door closed but the quaestor cuffed her.

Henghist, she thought, trying not to panic. Do you know where you sent me? Was this your plan all along, after you'd been lying to me all my life? Henghist.

She was led through a marbled hallway with discrete statutes, past a central atrium, and into another marbled room. There was a mosaic on the floor and a stone chair; several couches. She was forced onto her knees.

The room was cold and statue-less. She turned her head but Helvellyn growled at her.

There were footsteps in the hallway. Sandals on marble.

She raised her head as the man came into view. Helvellyn could have been her son, age-wise. The man had flame red hair, turning gold on top. Where Helvellyn was stout and grim faced, this man, the commander she presumed, was thin and fair skinned.

'Commander Valconius,' Helvellyn confirmed her guess, 'I arrested this druid in the forum.'

Valconius was studying her closely. He strode over.

'Sir, she is a –'

Valconius gripped her chin and lifted her head, tilting it this way and that. His fingers pinched but there was something in his gaze as he studied her intently.

'Sir?' asked Helvellyn.

Valconius shook his head, releasing her and stepping back. 'I am fine, quaestor. She has cast no enchantment on me.'

He continued studying her face.

'She is a druid –'

Valconius nodded absently. 'She resisted arrest, no doubt.'

Helvellyn glared at her. 'She attempted to escape. She questioned the nature of discipline in the forum.'

'Only because you –'

Helvellyn went for his gladius, but the black cloaked soldiers were faster. A pair of blades stopped an inch from the quaestor's face.

'You will not draw a weapon in my house quaestor.' Valconius sighed. 'It is only because I would not show you up by refusing you admittance with a sword that you have one. But do not presume to reach for it in my presence.'

He turned back to her. 'You almost – you –' he shook his head. 'Have you a brother?'

'No.' Jacaranda answered. 'I was an only child.' She frowned. I think. How can I not know?

There was a bang as the outer door was flung open. Both soldiers moved to face the open door. Helvellyn moved to one side, out of sight of anyone entering the room.

A ragged looking man appeared in the doorway. The soldiers sheathed their weapons. Valconius waved Helvellyn out of his place of hiding.

'What is it, Cleopatrius?'

The bearded man, who looked like one of the homeless from her Reading, pushed past the soldiers and gazed at her: dropped to his knees. 'I bring a message from the Oracle.'

Despite the sores on his face and the poverty of his clothing, his voice was strong.

Valconius nodded, glancing at her. 'What is it? Does it concern my prisoner?'

Cleopatrius stretched out on the marble full length towards her. Helvellyn gasped and Valconius raised an eyebrow. She looked at the commander, trying to work out what it meant.

'Hail, Caesar Jakanda.'

The soldiers became even more alert. Valconius was nodding, scrutinising her face intently. Helvellyn was scowling.

'Is that the Oracle's message?' Valconius asked.

Cleopatrius nodded, crawling backwards to the door. Jacaranda looked around. None of them were looking at her. If I bolted now, could I get through the door? If I could get to the housing blocks the bookshop appeared in –

'Leave us, quaestor.'

Helvellyn scowled harder, moving reluctantly. The black cloaked soldiers moved with him, inclining their heads slightly, she noticed, towards her.

The outer door opened. Closed.

Jacaranda looked up at Valconius. 'I'm not who you think I am.'

He nodded, waving her to silence as he went out to the hallway. He was back an instant later and drew her to her feet. He moved behind her; she felt his hand on her arm, tight for a moment. Tears pricked her eyes. Then the ropes were parting, falling away, and the pain as the blood flowed was worse.

'My name is Jacaranda. I –' she hesitated, lights dancing before her eyes, uncertain how to broach the rest of her tale.

Valconius nodded. 'Commander Jakanda. There were –' a faint flush of colour touched his cheeks. 'There were rumours, whispers, about your sex. But after ad Salices, no one questioned. You saved the Roman Empire at the Battle of Willows. You turned the barbarian tide. For the first time in nearly three thousand years we trembled. And you made us stand firm again.'

He grasped her hand and shook it enthusiastically. Then his expression changed and he pulled his hand away. 'I am sorry, Commander. That was overly familiar of me.'

Jacaranda shook her head. 'No, you don't understand. My name is Jacaranda and I'm from –'

Valconius nodded, sadness in his eyes. 'I understand that at the Battle of Willows you lost your son.' He sighed. 'I have no son, but I understand it is hard for a father to lose his son. How much harder it must be for a mother to lose her son. Your –' he hesitated, 'your withdrawal from public life, from the army, is most understandable.'

She shook her head but he pressed on.

'We know as well that you became – withdrawn from all aspects of reality. Some said you committed suicide. Some said you gibbered in a cell beneath the hills of Rome, mad and desolate beyond comprehension.'

Jacaranda sighed. 'I'm not. How can I –'

Valconius nodded, clapping his hands. 'I forget my manners, Commander Jakanda. My household is yours to command. You must be tired. I apologise for not thinking of it earlier. What do you require? A bath? Food? I will arrange for a medic, and fresh clothes, obviously.'

Some part of her rebelled, or maybe threw in the towel. 'A bath. And food.' She winced. 'Yes to a medic. And then a long sleep.'

He escorted her out and down the hallway to a room near the back of the house. A wave of heat rolled out as he opened the door.

An immense, low bath filled the room, with a pair of steps leading down. Racks of towels were dotted about the otherwise empty room. It's larger than most swimming pools she thought.

'It's the height of technology,' Valconius boasted, 'heated by the hypocaust. I'll send a serving girl in to wait on you.' He turned and flashed her a look somewhere between a grin and a leer. 'Or I have some young male servants who could cater to your each – and any – whim.'

Jacaranda blushed. 'I don't really –'. Seeing his frown, she changed her mind. 'A serving girl will be fine. My tastes are –' her blush deepened, 'only for food.'

Valconius nodded. 'Of course, Jakanda. I will leave you to bathe and relax. The girl will be in shortly to scrub your back and serve you food and anything else you require. I will arrange extra security while you are here. If you will excuse me –' he bowed and withdrew.

Jacaranda removed her jacket and sat on the edge of the bath. The water was warm, free flowing, constantly being refreshed. She held her head in her hands but it hurt.

'They think I'm someone I'm not. I can't tell him.' She sighed. 'If I play along, I'll get my chance.'

She undressed and shuffled into the pool. The steps continued: she found she could sit half way down, head on the steps, with the water coming up to her chest. The warmth eased some of the tightness, the trepidation, she had felt.

Henghist. How is this possible? She closed her eyes, letting her thoughts drift out across the water.

'Mistress.'

Jacaranda opened her eyes in alarm. A young girl, no more than sixteen or seventeen, knelt on the edge of the pool.

'I didn't hear you come in.'

'You were resting,' the girl said. 'May I feed you or scrub your back?' She gestured to the plates of food on the edge of the pool. There were cuts of meat, fresh fruit and soft, warm rolls.

Jacaranda shook her head. 'I can feed myself.' Bathing with Henghist had always ended a certain way, with banged heads and bruised hips and water all over the floor. If we'd had a pool like this – 'no.' She shook her head firmly, but smiled at the girl. 'I can bathe myself.'

The girl looked upset, nervous, but tried to mask it. 'As you wish, mistress.'

'What's wrong?' She caught the girl's wrist. 'My name's Jacaranda. What's yours?'

'Marcellina, mistress.'

'What will happen, Marcellina, if you return to Valconius?'

Marcellina bowed her head. 'He is a good master, mistress. He likes his guests to be properly looked after. He does not force us to do that which we do not want to, often. But we are his servants.'

Jacaranda snorted. Just as I was beginning to enjoy it. Rather Valconius than Helvellyn though. He would happily have killed or – she shuddered at the thought of Helvellyn.

'What's wrong, mistress?'

She smiled. 'I will not have you in trouble Marcellina. You can wash my hair if you will; feed me some choice titbits.'

The girl smiled broadly. 'Thank you, mistress. I will look after you. The medic will be in here shortly.'

Jacaranda closed her eyes. This is better than a health spa. Marcellina's hands were gentle as she rubbed water into her hair, then a mixture that smelt of honey. Occasionally a grape or a slice of apple or orange touched her lips and she took them gratefully.

'Mistress?'

She opened her eyes at the strange voice. A woman knelt beside the pool, older, grey haired, a shallow bowl in front of her filled with a paste of some sort.

'I am Quianna. I am the medic. Let me tend to your bruises.'

Jacaranda nodded, closing her eyes again and sinking deeper into the water until only her head was above.

The paste was cold, but soothing, applied to each bruise on her face.

'Try not to let water touch it,' Quianna instructed.

The door opened and closed: the medic was gone. The water was balmy, no less so for the length of time she'd spent in the pool. She lay with her head on Marcellina's shoulder; Marcellina's hands were linked below her chest and the water was doing warm, slow, dangerous things to her resistance.

Why was it never like this with Henghist? Why did nudity and water always lead to sex? She sighed. Because when I saw him naked I wanted him and when he saw me naked he never laughed.

'Are you alright, mistress?'

She hummed, not wanting to disturb the tranquillity.

'I came to tell you your room was ready, commander.'

Jacaranda opened her eyes and struggled to sit up, Marcellina still half clinging to her. Valconius was standing on the edge of the pool.

'Valconius.' She covered her chest hastily, then realised the water was clear: covered her sex one handed. 'Is that any way –'

The commander frowned. 'It has always been the custom in the Roman Empire for men and women to bathe together. Only in some backward, unenlightened, tribes is nakedness an issue.' His frown deepened. 'I have accorded you all the respect the holder of a grass crown can have; I can show you no more.'

She felt Marcellina disentangling herself hastily, as if burned.

'I do not understand your attitudes, Jakanda, though I do marvel the authenticity of your sex remained secret so long. How did you preserve it on the march and in camp?'

She stared at him, furious and impotent.

After a moment he shrugged. 'No matter.' He inclined his head. 'Your room is ready. Marcellina will cater for you during your stay. In the morning do you wish to go hunting or review the troops?' He half smiled. 'The inspection would do them good, and to know that Commander Jakanda has returned from the wilderness –'. The warmth in his eyes was unmistakeable.

Jacaranda lowered her arm, though she clenched one fist with the other. Valconius didn't so much as blink or drop his gaze from hers. 'My apologies, commander. As you said, it has been a long time. The wilderness –' she trailed off.

Valconius smiled warmly. 'I look forward to hearing your tale, when you are ready to tell it. And I apologise if I scared or startled you. I am honoured that you chose me; that you chose my town to return to.'

He bowed and withdrew. Jacaranda waited until the door had closed before turning round. Marcellina was looking up at her in awe.

'You have been awarded the grass crown, mistress?'

She nodded slowly. 'That's what Valconius said, isn't it? I'm rather tired now: I'd like to go to my bed.' And think about how to get out of here.

Marcellina scampered across the floor and fetched a towel. Started to –

'I can dry myself, Marcellina. You're shivering. Dry yourself.'

Clothing had been put out for her. There seemed a lamentable lack of recognisable underwear. Three thousand years of Empire and they haven't invented bras. Or television. Or cars. She grinned. Maybe it's not all bad.

Dressed, Marcellina led her to a chamber across the hallway. An opulent king sized bed in a large room. A fire burned in the grate.

'Mistress?'

She glanced at the girl, wondering if she'd somehow committed another faux pas.

'Some guests like me to sleep outside the door, to stop drafts. Others like me to stay by the fire, to keep it fed all night.'

Jacaranda snorted, shaking her head. 'How old are you, Marcellina?'

The girl raised her chin, aware she was being studied. 'Seventeen, mistress.'

So young. Could have been my daughter, if Henghist and I had been able – she shook her head. 'No. I just want to sleep, and I'm not putting you out. The bed is large enough. Plenty to share.' She mock frowned. 'As long as you don't steal the covers.'

Marcellina looked horrified. 'No, mistress, I wouldn't. A servant who stole would be whipped. Valconius is a good master.'

'I didn't mean that.' She shook her head. 'Never mind. Come on.'

The bed was warm. The room was warm, even without the fire. She undressed and slid in. Marcellina got in the other side. Jacaranda supposed the girl was attractive. About the age I was when Henghist – she cut the thought off. But seventeen and a slave. If I am – if they believe I am this commander – can I change things? Make it better for her and other slaves. That legionnaire that Helvellyn was punishing.

She turned onto her side. Marcellina wriggled over. She let the girl stretch her left arm out beneath her: laid her head on the girl's upper arm. The girl's right hand slid over her hip onto her belly. She drew Marcellina's hand up to her ribs. Marcellina moved, her right knee pressed against her thighs.

Jacaranda moved her right leg. Marcellina snuggled in tighter, until she could feel the girl's breasts flattened against her back, her breath warm on her neck.

Henghist, she thought sleepily. You might have dreamed of this, but you would never have understood. It's not sexual.

Marcellina's fingertips brushed the underside of her breast. 'Mistress.'

'Sleep,' she whispered. 'Just sleep.'

Marcellina eased back. Jacaranda let blissful sleep take her over.

--

There was something in the distance. A sunrise through a dark tunnel. It was only a short distance away. She only had to take the first step. The first step – she half moved her feet.

She wanted to turn her head. It felt like abandonment. But the sunrise was calling, was drawing her in. She'd be warm forever. Safe. No one would ever harm her again. No one would ever lie to her again.

Henghist. He'd lied to her. Would have gone on lying, if his hand hadn't been forced. Henghist. She wasn't going to let him get away with it. She turned her back on the sunrise.

--

There were hands around her throat. She drew a breath and failed. Her larynx was being crushed. There was a weight on her body, holding her down. Knees on her stomach.

She forced her eyes open.

Marcellina was bent over her, kneeling on her, hands round her throat.

She closed her eyes again. She felt weak, but knew she'd only get one chance. The girl's hands gripped too tightly. She was wrapped in the bedclothes, pinned beneath her: couldn't roll out from underneath.

She knew what she had to do but hesitated.

There were shouts in the distance. The clash of steel. Marcellina's fingers gripped even tighter.

Jacaranda gargled, her cry cut off, and scratched at the girl's cheeks.

Marcellina twisted, leaning forwards, forcing air out of her lungs: her left hand went wide. But she drew blood with her right.

Marcellina gasped, clutching her cheek. Jacaranda coughed and choked, struggling to breathe.

The door flew open, banging off the wall.

Marcellina turned, moving off her. Helvellyn stood in the doorway. Jacaranda felt her heart sink, but forced herself to open her eyes.

The servant leapt for the quaestor, but it was foregone: she stumbled and slid off him, impaled on his sword.

Helvellyn snatched up a dress and flung it at her. 'Get dressed, you stupid bitch. Valconius wants to kill you.'

The sounds of fighting drew nearer. Jacaranda fumbled with the clothing. Her fingers felt unconnected.

Cursing, Helvellyn took it off her and practically rammed it down onto her. 'No time.' He brushed aside her half formed pleas for respite, for slowing down. 'Valconius is jealous. He won't let you survive.' He grabbed her by the arm and tore her out of bed.

She stumbled and fell, bumping into Marcellina's corpse and screaming, though no sound left her throat. Her fingers were sticky with the girl's blood. The girl who'd bathed her, who'd washed her hair. She managed to shake her head, though the pain made her grimace. The girl who'd nearly strangled her.

Helvellyn pulled her to her feel. 'Run. Or do I need to carry you?'

She took halting steps. Feeling was returning to her legs. Her neck felt like it was aflame, inside and out. Her belly burned where Marcellina had knelt on her, but she managed to increase her pace as the quaestor tugged her along.

Valconius and three black cloaked guards were fighting against five of Helvellyn's men. As she saw them, a red cloaked soldier fell.

'Don't let her escape,' Valconius screamed, 'she'll put us all on charges. She's a traitor. A druid.'

Helvellyn dragged her away as his guards flung themselves at the commander.

'How?' she managed to ask.

A figure burst from a doorway, rolling pin in hand. Helvellyn cut them down without pausing.

'The Oracle.' Helvellyn dragged her towards the doorway, which stood ajar, red and black cloaked Roman soldiers spilled around it. 'Since Caesar Phillipius became ill, all the commanders have been jostling for power. Valconius is top dog: you threatened that.'

Jacaranda managed to shake her head without inflaming her headache too much. 'Who? Don't you serve him?'

Helvellyn snorted, dragging her south and east. She let him lead: it was in the right direction for the bookshop.

'I serve Rome. I serve the Roman Empire. You saved us once, Jakanda. You can again. If Valconius becomes emperor,' he shuddered, 'he is ruthless and charming, but mainly ruthless.'

They were heading down her street. Market Place, except here it was houses, apart from one grimy, boarded up window and a doorway no one mentioned, no one went through.

She dug her heels in, resisting.

Helvellyn scowled, pulling harder. 'Come on woman. My men didn't die so we'd be caught here. Valconius has brought the XIX up secretly: one of his guards escaped. We've got to get out of the town. Now.'

Jacaranda shook her head. 'I need to go in there. I've a way out of here.'

Helvellyn sighed, shaking his head. 'The Oracle didn't say you were a headstrong idiot. Valconius' guards will tear the building down to get at you.'

Jacaranda glanced at the doorway. There was light within, but too dim to see the lobby. It was so close. And Henghist, who'd sent her through – no. Who'd invited her to go through. To see for herself. To realise he wasn't lying about it, that he wasn't making it all up. Knowing she would accept. And it had nearly killed her.

She pulled her hand free of Helvellyn. She swallowed. It was like drinking dry fire. 'Thank you, Helvellyn, but this isn't my world. I'm not your Commander Jakanda. My name is Jacaranda. I run this shop – it's a bookshop. I'm a bookseller, not some famous war hero.'

He shook his head. She started to speak, but he held up his hand to stop her. 'The Oracle said I wouldn't understand. The Oracle said you would leave me and I couldn't follow.'

She touched the door handle. It twisted open easily: warmth flowed through her. 'I cannot help you, Helvellyn. Flee. Thank you for rescuing me, but don't die for it.'

He nodded, seizing her hand, kissing it and moving back. 'I will go. I still have some contacts. But the Oracle,' he paused. 'The Oracle said you would become the person the Empire thinks you are.' He grinned. 'Maybe you are not yet the person the Empire recognises.'

Jacaranda stared. 'Who is this oracle?'

Shouts at the far end of the street made him look away for an instant. 'I'd best be going. Whatever, however, you're going, I'd do it now.' He turned and ran.

Jacaranda stepped through the lobby door of her bookshop and closed it firmly.

God²

Courtney awoke when it was evening. The sun cast blood red shadows through the half-drawn curtains. He raised his head and groaned. The bookcase was leaning at an angle. A dozen or more CDs were scattered next to the docking station. A greasy plethora of chip papers spilled across the low table and a bottle of wine stood open.

He pulled himself out of bed, staggering through to the bathroom and gagging. All the bottles of Marie's, all that she'd not bothered with when she'd dumped him, had been opened and tried on. So was his aftershave and shower gel. The sink was slippery with cream and fragrance and oil.

He closed his mouth, pinching his nose as he turned the taps on. The bath looked worse. Streaks of purple and yellow were smeared across it; here and there cream and toothpaste had been splattered.

The water ran cold. He forced himself up, limbs protesting, to check the boiler. Stone cold, he muttered. He flicked water in his face, flinching. There were no clean towels. His hair was a mess; he ran damp hands through it.

'What? What happened?'

He went back to the bed-sitting room. T shirt and trousers were slung over the end of the bed. He pulled them on, finding clean socks in the cupboard. He hunted around, finding a clock.

'Half six. Saturday. What the –'

Courtney sat on the edge of the bed, closing his eyes. I was at work yesterday. Did we go for a drink? Why am I so tired? So knackered.

Sleep beckoned but he shook himself. Stood up. Something cracked. He looked down. A CD cover – Valentine

Wolfe – was broken. He pushed it aside, hunting for keys and shoes.

It was cold outside, colder than he'd expected. He crossed the Oxford Road, visiting the petrol filling station for junk food and cigarettes.

He crossed back again, ignoring the cars that tooted at him, and ripped open the packet of cigarettes.

'They'll kill you, you know.'

Faces, bodies, people, loomed out of the darkness. The speaker was Eastern European by his accent; a pair of Jamaicans and a couple of Asians backed him up.

Oh, shit. I've heard – I never thought – I always seemed –

They closed in on him.

--

Courtney awoke when it was evening. The sun cast blood red shadows through the half-drawn curtains. The air was fetid, thick, stale.

He pulled himself out of bed. Everything had been opened in the bathroom – all of Marie's beauty products were cast about, smeared on the walls and in the bath.

He frowned, running the bath taps. The overpowering scents were making his eyes water: he splashed water in them; ran his hands through his hair.

He went back to the other room and dressed. There was nothing in the fridge, not even the ice cream, he was sure had been unopened. The petrol filling station was close by. He headed over, buying fags as well.

'They'll kill you, you know.'

Five people – muggers – were closing in on him. He gripped the carrier bag. As weapons went, it was fairly useless.

'Or they would,' the speaker continued in a heavily accented voice, 'if we weren't going to.'

Knives glinted in the darkness. He tried to back away. A hand touched his back.

--

Courtney awoke when it was evening. The sun cast blood red shadows through the half-drawn curtains. He frowned, rubbing his brows.

'What the –'

The room was a tip. The bathroom even more so. He flicked water in his face to wake himself up, dressed and went out.

The clerk in the service station smiled blandly, returning his card as he shovelled the food into the bag, the pack of cigarettes going in his pocket.

'They'll kill you, you know.' The gang leader grinned. 'Or they would, if we weren't going to.'

He backed away. A hand touched his back and he froze.

'This is your only warning. Why do you – gentlemen – not desist, and leave Courtney alone.'

He half turned his head but stopped as the five fanned out. The speaker behind him was a woman; strange lilt to her voice.

The leader laughed, the others smirking. 'Don't interfere, girlie. No one extra has to be hurt beyond Mr Courtney. It's only him we're after.'

The woman snorted. 'I warned your paymaster not to interfere.'

The leader frowned. 'In that case –'

He rushed forwards, blade raised. Courtney backed away, tripping and falling heavily. When he looked up, the woman was standing over the body of the gang leader. Blood was pooling beneath his chest.

'You've – you've –' Courtney turned his head and threw up.

The four closed in.

--

Courtney awoke when it was evening. Feeling terrible and desperately hungry, he dressed and went to the service station.

'They'll kill you, you know.'

He clutched at the cigarettes. Everything was fuzzy. Familiar.

'This is your only warning. Why do you gentlemen not desist and leave Courtney alone.'

The woman knew his name. He shuddered, moving back, falling, as she moved forwards. There was a cry. A terrible wet sound. Courtney threw up.

He wiped his mouth. When he could he looked up. Three of the men were down. One was gasping, clutching his stomach. Blood pooled around the other two. The remaining two would-be muggers closed in on his saviour. There was a whistling sound. A thud. The fourth fell.

The last launched himself at her. She half turned. Caught the attacker's wrist and twisted. Courtney grimaced, feeling his stomach heave as he heard the crack.

And then the muggers were all down and she was turning back to face him.

'Why do I keep remembering –'

--

Courtney awoke when it was evening. The room, the bathroom, the attempted mugging –

'Why do I keep remembering?'

She drew him up. Her skin was pale brown, cinnamon brown. Her eyes were shadowed but shone brightly, impossibly, lime green. Her black hair was pulled back in a plait. She was so plain and unadorned – no rings, no makeup – that he felt his heart lurch.

'You are safe. I should –'

94

He put his arm round her waist and pulled her closer. She was warm and he could taste her perspiration on the night air and she wasn't exactly resisting, but neither was she compliant.

'You saved me. Those muggers –' he stared at her. 'They knew me. They were after me.'

Courtney staggered. Her arm was round his waist, supporting him. He drew her closer. Could feel her thigh pressed against his. The warmth of her body; the strength of her arms as she held him.

Her hand guided his to put the key in the lock. He wasn't drunk but she was intoxicating. He was glad he'd vacuumed that morning.

She looked around in bright eyed wonder. She was slim; petite. A little over 5'3" he guessed, and so different from Marie.

'I wanted to thank you.'

She didn't resist as he pulled her into his embrace. Returned his kiss warmly. Her hands were tugging at his trousers. He tugged at her blouse and she broke the kiss so he could pull it over her head.

--

He only remembered to ask her name the third time he woke in her embrace.

--

'Chin-gáro.'

He was lying on his side, admiring her; she lay on her back.

'Chin-gáro.' He traced lazy spirals on her stomach. 'Where does the name come from?'

She shrugged sweetly. 'I do not know. I did not know my parents.' She looked around. 'Is this your house, Courtney?'

He nodded, his fingers creeping downwards.

'May I look around?'

She slipped out from underneath him and padded over to the bookcase. In the streetlight that spilled through the open curtains her body was very pale, with dark, impenetrable shadows. She ran her fingers up and down book spines. Drew one out and sniffed it. Pressed it against her cheek.

'Chin-gáro?'

She opened the book and cried out. A drop of blood welled up on her finger. Before he could move, she popped it in her mouth, returning the book and choosing another.

'Do you always sniff books?'

She turned to face him, removing her finger and opening the book she'd chosen carefully. 'I have only seen parchment before. This —'

Courtney swallowed, watching the emotions that played across her face as she ran fingers over the pages. Will she ever look at me like that?

'Have you heard music?' he asked, slipping out of bed.

She frowned, looking around the room. 'Of course I have. But you have no instrument.' She clapped her hands, smiling. 'Oh. You are a singer.'

Courtney grinned, shaking his head. 'No. Let me show you.'

He pulled a couple of CDs out of the rack, abandoned them, and found his MP4 player. Music swirled across the room, spacey electronica. Chin-gáro had her head tilted back to listen, eyes half closed, a smile playing across her lips.

'This is like the music of the wind,' she said, 'when it takes you to the place of dreams.'

He found the original CD and passed it to her. She looked at the circular disc. Sniffed it. Licked it. Frowned. Pulled the lyric sheet out, but dropped it just as quickly.

'What's wrong?'

'It is.' She frowned. 'It feels smooth. It does not feel like parchment.'

His stomach rumbled. Chin-gáro looked up and smiled. 'Are you hungry?' he asked.

She nodded, running her fingers along the edge of a slipcase.

Courtney fetched the mint ice cream and a pair of spoons.

Chin-gáro seemed taken with the plastic container and would have licked it had he not fed her. She took the spoon from him and licked it clean; got another scoop. She stared at him openly, appraisingly, while she licked the spoon again. Her lips were pale; almost bloodless.

He kissed her again, tasting the mint in her breath.

'Chin-gáro. How did you know my name? Why were those muggers trying to kill me?'

--

He went out and bought some fish and chips and a bottle from the corner shop. Chin-gáro had seduced him after he'd asked the question. He'd left her having a bath.

Who is she? Why did she save me – and what happened to the muggers? Courtney passed the place it had happened. There was no blood. No police tape. No boards requesting witnesses to come forwards.

'Chin-gáro?'

The house smelt overpowering as he opened the front door.

Chin-gáro came out of the bathroom, her hair wrapped in a towel, smelling of conflicting herbal essences and mineral extracts. Through the open door he could see she'd been playing with all the pots and jars Marie had left; all the things he'd meant to throw out, but put off because it was all he had left from that relationship.

'Chin-gáro,' he said gently, then remembered the muggers she'd killed. 'I want answers. Who are you – really? How do you know me? How did they, and why are they trying to kill me?'

She took a step closer, crooning low in the back of her throat. He shook his head.

'No, Chin-gáro. Get dressed. Tell me. Please. I want to know what's going on.'

She sighed. 'It will be better if you do not ask this. Please. I will do anything for you.' Chin-gáro smiled, her look lascivious. 'Anything.'

He gathered up her clothes and tossed them to her. Reluctantly, a little sadly he thought, she took them.

Chin-gáro dressed, then sat amid the scattered CDs. 'I do not have parents. I have names for parents, but that is all. They are not real people. I was trained as a scholar, but I came here.'

He started to ask but she held up her hand to forestall him.

'I came from a poor area. I overcame adversity. I was called urchin and doxy by those who should have respected me.' She raised and studied her hand. 'But there was no – progress. No room to grow.' She smiled. 'And now –'

Courtney shook his head, but she stopped him with a look. He shivered. Did she give that same look to those muggers?

'I am your creation. I am alive. Truly alive.' She shook her head. 'And it is terrible and beautiful and thrilling and so terrifying and I am alone.'

He stared. 'What do you mean – 'I am your creation'?'

Chin-gáro looked up at him, a tear in her eye. 'You will write a story. And then another. And another. I am your central character.' She shook her head. 'But something went wrong.'

'What? Don't be – you can't –'

'Someone is trying to kill you.' She stared at him with her curious and electrifying green eyes. 'Because I am here, they have not yet succeeded. If they succeed, I fail to exist. If I fail to protect you, you fail to create me. You die.' She shook her head. 'I am only a work of fiction, but you –'

'No, Chin-gáro.' Courtney crossed to her and took her hands. 'You're wrong. You can't be. It doesn't happen.' He snorted. 'Certainly not in Oxford Road.'

She shook her head, reaching out to touch his cheek. 'I did not want to – I wanted to resist you. I should have.' She shook her head. 'But I am glad I did not. How else would you have come up with my exploits?'

Courtney shook his head. 'You're – confused. Delirious. You can't be – I –'

'Do you deny you write?'

He snorted. 'Of course not. But –'

'But nothing. You will create me because you have created me. I am your progeny. Your daughter. Your lover. Your muse. And,' she grinned suddenly, 'now, it appears, your bodyguard.'

Courtney pulled back from her, rubbing his hands. 'I created you? But then –' he felt sick.

She took his hands. 'You have always liked girls with green eyes. And since you were brought up in Asia you have a predisposition towards the Asian caste. You prefer your women –' she drew his hands to her chest, 'small and strong willed.'

Courtney pulled his hands away. 'No. Yes. No.' He shuddered, wiping his hands on his trousers. 'What I – what we – if you are –' he felt himself start to heave and got to his feet; ran for the bathroom.

My daughter. She. I. We. She was lying there, naked, inviting, inspiring. He threw up again.

A cool hand mopped his brow. Lifted him. Guided him through to the bedroom.

'Sleep. I will watch. It will be better in the morning.'

--

Courtney awoke when it was evening. The sun cast blood red shadows through the half-drawn curtains. He raised his head and groaned.

Extemporary in Arcadia

The young woman was sitting in the mouth of her cave, not crying, not moving, not doing anything. It was the third day she'd been there, her eyes open but unseeing.

Lakshmi moved up and sat cross legged beside her.

There were dried tears on the woman's face which had half dissolved the grime on her cheeks. There was a faint smell of milk, but nothing else. She put her hand on the woman's arm.

The woman raised her head, her neck stiff. Her eyes were dulled, blank, unseeing.

'Lakshmi.'

The sound of a voice, even one so raw, so broken, was surprising to Lakshmi. She had lived in silence all her life.

The woman had lowered her gaze again, sitting on her knees, her hands palm up, fingers curled. She came from the village someways down the mountain, Lakshmi knew.

She'd fashioned a porch out of wood, four cornered and square, that she might sit in the sun and meditate. She didn't speak, she didn't eat, she only drank water in the depths of winter. The sun and the stars provided all she needed.

But this villager sat in her cave, not her porch, and for two days she'd barely noticed her. The sun warmed her. It gave her all she needed. A remote spot in which to meditate. Her children, twins, were long gone, gone to Kathmandu to study, and she had moved from the village where she'd come into being.

She had passed through the village once, far below, many years ago. Her passing had been remarked upon, but she had sought only the warmth of the sun and the caress of the wind and the cool of the night. She had no crops to plant: no need for crops.

Lakshmi had tried to be forgotten.

She touched the woman's arm again and studied her face when she raised her gaze. The young woman's eyes were dark, heavy with unwept tears. Her clothing was old, worn, but she was still young. Not more than eighteen. Probably no more than sixteen.

'Lakshmi,' the woman's voice cracked, was younger.

She stroked the woman's arm sympathetically. Life in remote villages was hard. What did she know? What could she do to help? Nothing, and so she had avoided them. She didn't want another village trying to worship her.

'I.' The woman sniffed. 'I will not kill myself. But I will not eat. Why should I? What is there?'

Her hands had the beginnings of calluses: she worked in the fields so the family could survive.

Lakshmi closed her eyes. Her children had everything, the villagers had given them everything. The villagers had thought her a Goddess. The villagers had almost made themselves poor in their adoration of her, of them, the children of a Goddess.

The girl clenched her fists. 'I could not stay. Sunil is dead. How can I go on? I have no dowry. No man will take me.'

Lakshmi touched her own breast and pointed at the girl.

She sniffed louder. 'Angeli. I cannot feed her. I am dust. Ash. If Sunil had lived –' she looked down again.

Lakshmi didn't know how long she'd lived in the cave. How long she would have to live before she met the man again, the man who had cared for her in the village where she came to, the man whose voice had sent her consciousness into the stars and whose touch had grounded her.

She couldn't imagine what it would be like to never hear him again, to never feel his gentle touch on her body.

She rose and began walking.

The skirt rustled around her ankles. The sun warmed her body even as the wind tickled it. She could smell the coldness in the air. Winter was coming on.

She knew where the village was. It was a good half a day's distance, but time seemed fluid. The village was just – there.

She could smell the gasoline and incense, the cow dung and the dahl bhat all overlaid and intermingled with the scents of humans.

Lakshmi walked into the village. Most villagers were working in the fields, their cries strident in the afternoon air. Here and there a toothless shadow of a person peered at her from the darkness of the mud baked houses. A few voices whispered her name.

She knew which was the woman's house. It stood a little apart, newer, but already falling derelict. She had to bend low to step inside.

The cooking fire was long dead. Meat hung from the ceiling, cracked and dried. The house was lifeless –

Lakshmi turned.

A bundle on the floor shifted, kicked a tiny foot. She crossed to it and sat beside the baby. They were only a few months old, thin and starved and close to death.

She peeled the swaddling and lifted the baby to her breast. Angeli didn't want to feed, but Lakshmi pushed her nipple against the girl's mouth until she began to investigate.

'Lakshmi.'

She turned. One of the elder womenfolk of the village knelt in the doorway. 'Life was hard for Srijana. When Sunil died –'. She sighed. 'We cannot lose a young woman but we cannot support her.'

Lakshmi stroked Angeli's head. The baby girl nuzzled contentedly, little more than a sack of bones, but still alive, still fighting for a chance.

She remembered how healthy her children were; how any child she'd nursed became fitter, hardier.

Lakshmi took one of the dozen necklaces she wore and gave it to the woman. The necklace was adorned with lapis lazuli and black diamonds. The woman's eyes bulged: she made to refuse. Lakshmi indicated the house, that she would support the infant. The woman took it, concealing it on her person and withdrew.

She looked down at Angeli. There was life in the baby girl's eyes. While there was life – she stroked the girl's cheek – there was still time.

Theoythric

The hills of Leaford had never looked so green. Rain fell in fine, slanting lines, but seemed to sparkle and diminish in the bold sunlight. The rill, marking the northern edge of her property, flowed swiftly. A bird chirruped a damp, enquiring chirp.

Marian smiled fondly. She turned back from the window and sat down in the chair her serving woman had prepared for her. It was deep and lined with furs, warm despite the turn of the year.

Robin nuzzled hungrily at her breast. He was only six months old but growing fast. She held him with one arm beneath him, the other around his back. He suckled eagerly, one hand up beside his mouth, his other outflung. His hair was fine, blond, his blue eyes sparkling just like his father's.

Her serving woman had been horrified.

'It would never have happened in your father's time, God rest his soul. You're lucky Sir Guy let –'

Lucky. Marian stroked her son's cheek. She was lucky. Guy had protected her interests after her father died on the Crusades. He hadn't had to, but they had drawn close. He had continued the weapons' training her father had started, until she could outshoot any of his verderers. He had often taken her hunting, using a lodge of his hidden deep in the Royal Forest.

She had shot the deer and he had cooked it for them, feeding her pieces of the rich, privileged venison, which both of them could lose their lives for hunting.

He had made a private display of chastising her later, putting her across his knee and lifting her skirts. But after that his hand had dipped lower and she'd been delighted by the feelings he'd aroused and that night, in the warmth and safety of his lodge, they'd explored their feelings for each other.

After that he'd had her confirmed as lord of Leaford – lady, strictly, though it was little more than a draughty hall, a couple of farms and some rolling hillsides.

Marian moved Robin to the other breast. He objected being removed, no matter how gently, but abandoned his fears when his questing mouth found her nipple. Both his hands were on her breast as if to prevent it being removed again.

He'll be a hit with the girls when he's older, she thought warmly. He has his father's love of my body.

The sunlight streamed in warmly, hotly. She'd undone the bodice of her gown, and done without the ridiculous undergarments.

'My lady,' Beatrice, her serving woman had protested loudly, often, 'no lady feeds the child. That is what wet nurses are for.'

Marian had ignored her. Beatrice often protested – for the sake of protesting. She closed her eyes. Motherhood had made her appreciative of the lightest touch on her body and the sunlight and the taste of rain in the air and her son's mouth made her yearn for Guy to be present, to come visit her, visit her son.

Mostly she needed Guy to come and lay her down, to give her want she wanted – needed – from him.

But Guy was married and his wife had the ear of King Rufus and she was suspicious so Guy had to pay court to the older, raddled woman.

Robin burped and laid his head between her breasts. She stroked his back and the fine blond curls.

Marian opened her eyes at the sound of scurrying feet as Beatrice flew into the room.

'Oh – my lady – you cannot meet them like that – there are – gentlemen here.'

She heard the mailed feet on the stairs leading to the chamber and smiled.

'Guy?'

--

Guy knew he was in trouble.

'My wife –'

The Archbishop shook his head smugly. 'It was your wife who made us aware of your –' there was a knowing pause, 'tendencies.'

Guy frowned. 'My what?'

The Archbishop smiled a thin-lipped smile. 'Your father was under suspicion of being a Cathar. His heresy was – managed.'

'Managed?' Guy levered himself off the wall. 'He was tortured to death.'

The Archbishop's smile broadened. 'Isn't that your fondest desire? You believe this life is Hell and long for your soul to escape it.' He shook his head. 'You are fatally flawed and I regret that I must confirm your deepest, incorrect, spiritual wish, but it is for your own good. Your mortal soul may be saved before then, however.'

Guy closed his eyes. Agnes betrayed me. Black Agnes was always going to betray me. As long as Marian and little Robin remain free, my death will not be in vain.

Marian. The light of his life. Her father had been a Christian, but a good man. He had gladly extended his protection to her when Sir Leaford had died. There were too many greedy barons who would have cared nothing for a ten year old girl, only the land and property which was her father's gift to her.

He'd always liked her spirit, her fire, her, he wouldn't deny it, her body. Agnes was aged, shrivelled, uninterested unless it suited her. But Marian was a little younger than him, vibrant, laughing, joyous.

That time in the lodge – he'd only meant it teasingly, to begin with. But she hadn't objected when he'd slapped her backside lightly. She'd squirmed deliciously at his gentle chastisement. And so he'd explored, and she'd enjoyed and thus he'd betrayed Agnes and Marian had fallen pregnant.

'I hope you are not saying prayers. To commit heresy whilst being investigated for heresy –'

'Investigated?' Guy spat, blood in the phlegm. 'You're going to kill me because I'm a Cathar.'

The Archbishop placed his hand on Guy's head. 'Oh, my foolish child. You admit your sins – that is good. But heresy must be rooted out. We must know how far it has spread.'

The Archbishop pushed his head back against the wall. 'I do not enjoy my work. It is a necessary evil. But we must save who we can.'

Guy scowled.

'For instance. I have heard tale that this Marian of Leaford has recently born child.'

Guy clenched his teeth together and met the Archbishop's gaze unflinchingly.

'Women are necessary for the production of life; little else. Yet this Marian is unmarried. She compounds sin upon sin.'

'I know nothing of –'

'With the favour given you for your father's deeds and in his memory, you were able to get Marian confirmed as lord of Leaford. That suggests you do know.'

Guy bit his lips.

'Perhaps if she were brought in and put to the question.'

'Marian is not a Cathar.'

The Archbishop smiled blandly. 'I did not expect she was. But she has grievous sins upon her soul, and so do you, and the nearness of your estates cannot be overlooked.'

Guy shook his head.

'Evil takes root, Guy. It festers beneath the surface and takes different forms in different people. With you, it is Cathar heresy. With Marian, it is a Jezebellian whoredom.'

'Marian is no –'

'I shall be the judge of that. I sent for her a while ago. I will be – interested – to hear what she says.'

'No –'

The Archbishop chuckled, rapping on the cell door. 'I will return with her shortly. After I have been given some answers.'

Guy screamed in terror as the Archbishop left.

--

Archbishop Longranes smiled in true pleasure. He could appreciate why Guy had tumbled her. She was far more delectable that the English King's god-damned cousin Lady Agnes ever would have been.

But she is so beautiful she would put Mary, the mother of Christ, to shame, and so she must be punished for the sin of being attractive to a man's eye.

Shoulder length copper hair. A pleasingly expressive face, eyes a sea blue with the hint of green depths. Not as tall as a man – she did not have that arrogance, but broad shouldered.

Málefric, the leader of his guards, had reported that when they'd arrested her she'd been holding her child to her chest, wantonly bare breasted.

And why not Longranes thought, greedily devouring her appearance. Immoral, unchristian motherhood had made her as ripe and luscious as the fruit that tempted Eve. Long armed and supple handed. Not the hands of a lady.

'Where is my son? What have you done with him?'

Her belly was flat, softly rounded, punctured by the navel.

He backhanded her casually.

Muscled legs, the legs of one used to riding and being ridden.

'Who is the father of your bastard child?'

'I do not know his name. He was a trader –'

The knife blade was half as long as his middle finger. Even in that, it was often too much. But it slid in and out easily, leaving her gasping, bleeding.

'Do not lie, child. Your soul is all but damned for your carnality. Repent. Ease the burden.'

He punctured her navel and smiled as the blood ran down her belly.

'Please. I –'

'Tell the truth, child. Which man did you subvert? Whom did you ensnare between your whore's thighs?'

He pierced each thigh in turn. Marian was crying, gulping, but he paid no attention. The pin pricks were minor. The blood loss minor. Of all the women he'd questioned, none had died from the initial phase of enquiry.

'This does not have to hurt, child. Give up the man who forces me to do this. Give me a name.'

He plunged the thin bladed knife in and she gave a ragged scream.

'Surrender. The pain can stop. Give me a name or this will continue. I have no choice. God wills it.'

He drove the knife in, watching the blood flow as the sinner's screams intensified.

There was only so much he could do. After a while some sinners moved beyond the level of pain where driving a knife in would have any effect.

So it is with this whore. She must be well ridden to withstand such pain.

Longranes looked up at her face. He hadn't touched that yet, but –

'Tell me who your child's father is or I will harm the child.'

'No,' she screamed, thrashing in the chains, 'hurt me. Don't hurt Robin, please. If you have any compassion at all –'

'You care for Guy, do you not?'

She stared, blinking. 'What?'

'Tell me Guy is the father and you will be enquired of no more. I will not hurt or kill your child. Did Guy corrupt you? Was he the one who deflowered you of your sweet, Christian, innocence?'

'You promise?' she asked, her voice broken.

Longranes nodded. He placed the tip of the knife carefully against her breast. 'I will not harm or kill your son Robin, nor shall you be harmed anymore. This I swear by Our Lady,' and he pushed the knife slowly in.

'Guy,' she screamed, howling, thrashing in the chains. 'Guy is Robin's father.'

He pulled the knife out, wiping it on a blood-free part of her belly.

'Thank you, child. You could have saved yourself much pain had you told me earlier.'

He rapped on the cell door. 'And so we get closer to the truth which will save your souls.'

--

Déraciné stalked through Guiswardine castle, flanked by a pair of Gurkhas.

'Wrong, wrong, wrong,' he muttered. 'All wrong.'

He'd encountered Guy's verderers in the forest following the trail of the Archbishop's warriors who'd arrested Marian.

'They've arrested her, and the Archbishop's at Guiswardine and he'll have put her to the question.'

Judicious questioning had revealed the missing information, and he wouldn't have been interested but –

But Wizerbowski did say to lie low just in case, and a reality where the Crusades and the persecutions of the Cathars is conflated –

'She's not married but she has a child and she's a good bow –'

'No,' another verderer had interrupted, 'she's the best archer we've ever seen, particularly in a woman. She must have Welsh blood.'

Déraciné knew what he needed. A suitable base of operations. Guiswardine castle would be just that. He'd already brought through a few warriors, but to assemble an army, a host –

As if a host could hold off Armageddon. But I can offer the host to Jacaranda. It may not be too late to avert the Big Bang, as long as we can stop Henghist and Horsa.

He reached a fork in the passage and paused. One of the Gurkhas indicated right. He went right.

The passage wound down. There were fewer torches and more indiscernible stains on the stones.

A scream made his blood run cold.

A guard stood in front of the door ahead: the scream had come from within. 'You cannot,' he began, reaching for the sword at his waist but fell, a khukri in his chest.

The Gurkha retrieved his weapon, cleaning it on the Norman soldier's cloak, indicating there was one person inside.

The key was still in the lock. Déraciné glanced at his guards, then turned the key and flung the door open.

A figure turned. From the descriptions of rumours the verderers had given him, and from the haughty expression of his mien, Déraciné guessed it was the Archbishop. Grand Torturer, more like.

The Archbishop was dying, one khukri in his chest, the other in the base of his throat.

But the other two occupants of the room – Déraciné swallowed. I hope they died first. I hope –

The first was a tall, blond haired male, hanging blessedly dead in his chains. He was naked, his genitals hacked off. His head had fallen forwards, mouth open. The lower jaw was drenched in blood: the man's tongue had been ripped out.

Déraciné turned away and was sick.

A sound, movement, made him turn back.

A woman hung in the other chains. Naked, her body half drenched in blood. Her mouth opened. Something fell out.

For a moment Déraciné thought she'd had her tongue removed as well. Then he realised it was the man's tongue.

She moved in the chains. 'Kill me,' she cried.

'Fetch me one of the verderers. I think we've found Marian.'

One of the Gurkhas left, as silent as a shadow.

The woman moved again. Something fell from her, landing with a wet thump. The nobleman's severed manhood.

'Sweet Jesus. Marian. Guy.'

One of the verderers brushed past Déraciné. Turned away and was sick.

Déraciné stepped forwards. Lying on the floor beneath Marian was her child. He didn't need to look to know the boy child was dead.

'Kill me,' Marian murmured again. 'This is Hell and I want Guy's Heaven.'

He went to the verderer. 'Where is the man we caught?'

'Málefric? He's –'

'Málefric.' Marian raised her head, blood on her lips. 'He,' and she jerked her head at the Archbishop. 'He kept his word. He didn't kill Robin. He gave him to –' she broke off, crying.

Déraciné glanced at the Gurkhas. 'Cut her down, give her a weapon, bring this Málefric here.'

He took his jacket off and placed it over Marian's shoulders as she knelt clasping her son to her breast.

'Robin. Robin.'

She stayed there for fully ten minutes after the Gurkhas returned, dragging the Archbishop's captain of guards with them.

'When King Rufus hears of this – let alone the Holy Roman Empire –'

'You'll be long dead,' Déraciné finished curtly, 'and so will the whole universe and all realities unless we can prevent any more chronological anomalies.'

Marian moved. She laid Robin down gently, closing his eyes and kissing his forehead.

'Farewell, Robin. I love you. Guy loved you. We will always love you.'

She stood up, his jacket falling from her shoulders.

Déraciné stepped out of her way.

She brushed past the Gurkhas to stand face to face with Málefric.

'You murdered my son.'

He stared back. 'You were just a –'

Málefric was suddenly falling back, his chest a vivid red slash. Marian advanced, a Gurkha's blade in her hand.

The second blow emasculated the warrior. At the third he lost his head.

Déraciné turned away. There were wet, dripping sounds, and the sound of a cleaver hitting stone or carving through bone, but he made no attempt to stop Marian or to leave.

If I had watched. Listened. I would have seen Jacaranda was not the guilty one. I blew my chance. I will be lucky to get a second.

The sounds of futile vengeance died out. He heard Marian move but didn't turn back.

'Who are you?'

Marian was kneeling beside her son, wrapped in his jacket. Blood was splashed across her face and in her hair.

'My name is Déraciné,' he said, sinking to one knee, 'and I may have something for you to live for.'

The other Henghist

Jacaranda stepped through the lobby door of her bookshop and closed it firmly.

Except it wasn't the lobby and it wasn't her bookshop.

The vaulted dome of the roof was far above her, lined with beaten gold. Marble columns supported the ceiling and the walls were marble, interspersed with large, high, stained glass windows through which golden sunlight streamed.

Jacaranda swallowed. The dress was unfamiliar – she'd only worn a dress once before, at her wedding – and woollen and scratchy. She looked down. Barefooted as well, with grimy feet from running through the streets of the Roman Reading.

The walls were lined with books. Where she might have expected pews there were bookcases with low seats in front of them. Row upon row of bookcases with silent worshippers eagerly devouring the knowledge therein.

Jacaranda turned away. Henghist, why did you –

A figure caught her eye, striding up one side of the cathedral, books clamped beneath his arm.

She stared in disbelief.

Her disbelief lasted only a moment and then she was pounding across the marble, ignoring the scandalised glances being cast at her.

The man she was following had turned a corner and entered a maze of high, solid, bookcases.

'Henghist. I could have died –' she caught at his arm.

He spun round, the books flying from his grasp.

'Madam, I assure you –'

Jacaranda stared. It was Henghist. And it wasn't. The same dark hair, height, everything. But the look in his eyes was different.

'– I have never met you before and yet you know me. Is this some university prank? A jape, perhaps.'

She stared, shaking her head. 'No. No. You just reminded me of –'

'I hesitate to ask but at your age, madam –'

'My age?' Jacaranda bridled.

'I did not mean to give offense, madam; please forgive me. You do not look like a student. And yet you turn up in the library in disarray, missing shoes.' He shook his head. 'Was there drink or significant sums of money involved?'

She stared. 'Henghist. You're Henghist.'

The man – Henghist – nodded uncomfortably. 'Yes, madam. Henghist Goring. Named after the Norse invaders all those years ago. My mother had a thing for history.' He stared. 'I do not know you. Why am I telling you this?'

Jacaranda frowned. 'Do you have a brother named Horsa Streatley?'

Henghist nodded. 'The surnames were my father's choice. He wanted to add colour to the family tree.' He frowned.

Jacaranda shook her head. 'I married you. A different you.'

'I assure you, madam, I think I would remember.'

'Did your brother commit suicide?'

Henghist's face closed. 'I am sorry, madam. I think it would be better if you left the library.'

He took her by the arm.

'No, wait, Henghist. Mr Goring. Please. Let me explain.'

He stopped dragging her, though he didn't remove his hand.

'There is a doorway. It leads to my bookshop. But sometimes it leads – other places. I was running away from a Roman Empire of the 21st Century. When I woke up this morning a servant girl was trying to kill me and a commander thought I was a threat to his dreams of empire.'

Mr Goring released his hand. 'I think I was wrong to try and throw you out. I think –' he paused. 'You need support.'

Jacaranda shook her head. 'No. Listen, Henghist. I was – I am – I have been married to Henghist Goring for twenty-five years. He came from an alternate earth. He knew all about the different realities but kept it secret from me.'

He took a step back. 'I think –'

Jacaranda took a half step. 'Wait. Please. Let me ask you one thing.'

He nodded grudgingly.

'Do you remember, about twenty-seven, twenty-eight years ago –'

He snorted, scowling, but Jacaranda pressed on.

'The early eighties. You – my Henghist – went to a school disco.'

He scowled. 'It was the early eighties. New wave of romantic and all that. Everyone went to school discos.'

Jacaranda shook her head. 'There was a club. A young girl standing by the bar. Too shy, too unsure, to buy a drink or go onto the dance floor. You – my Henghist – asked me to dance.'

Henghist's eyes narrowed. 'There was a girl, propping the wall up. She looked self-contained.'

She shook her head again. 'She didn't know what to do. She didn't know anyone there.'

He thinned his lips. 'It could have been anyone.'

Jacaranda shrugged. 'The man I went on to marry asked me to dance. Bought me a drink. After the disco finished we went into the alley and,' she looked away. 'Well, I was no longer so unknowing. But he came back. Again and again. One day he told me we were marrying and I said yes.'

Henghist looked away, his eyes shadowed.

'For twenty- five years, the two of us were happily married –' she began.

'Are you telling me –' and Jacaranda was surprised at the anger, at the bitterness in his voice – 'that if I'd asked you to dance –'

Jacaranda shrugged.

Henghist snorted. 'Why couldn't you – or anybody – have told me that thirty years ago?' He shook his head wistfully. 'I never had the confidence with girls. I was always – shy.'

'You seem to have done alright.'

He snorted. 'I've never really –' he saw the look on her face. 'Oh. I'm not – innocent – but there's been no one long term. No special woman. I don't know how to –'

Jacaranda took his hands. 'You be yourself. With confidence and humour –'

She leant in and kissed him.

'This isn't really the place –'

Jacaranda drew back from him at the woman's voice.

'Oh. Curator. I didn't expect it to be you with this – woman.'

Jacaranda moved back, smoothing the dress down where it had ridden up, aware for the first time that she needed a bath.

'This is a friend of a cousin of mine, Elaine. She's in a spot of trouble. Please be discrete.'

The librarian, Elaine, gave her an unfriendly look and retreated back to the main body of the cathedral.

'That's the confidence you need, Henghist. You knew what to say.'

He blushed. 'It was – a bit like an adventure. I didn't even think.'

She smiled. 'I – I should really be going –'

'Would you like to go to the cinema?'

Jacaranda stared. Henghist was staring, in surprise she thought, at his own confidence, his own nerve.

'If I'm staying, then I need to – freshen up. Shoes would be good. And I want to change out of the dress.'

He half frowned. 'I – like the dress.'

She shook her head. 'It rides up too easily. I left in a hurry this morning. I didn't have time to –'

He stared at her for a moment, then blushed, realising what she meant. 'I can loan you – jeans. And things.'

An hour later she was standing in his bathroom combing her hair. She'd borrowed jeans, a T shirt and boxers off him.

'Are you ready, Jacaranda?' Henghist called up.

She left the bathroom and went downstairs. The flat was compact but beautifully furnished, if slightly unlived in.

'I say. That's an improvement.'

She smiled at his awkward compliment. He didn't appear to have changed his clothes, only his shoes.

'You're the curator of the library?'

Henghist nodded. 'It pays well, but without someone –' he clamped his mouth shut.

Jacaranda laughed, offering him her arm. 'Shall we go?'

Going to the pictures with Henghist – her Henghist, the lying, manipulative bastard – had always been an excuse for him to touch her up in public. They'd always taken the back row. His hand had always been inside her knickers before the adverts had even finished.

But this Henghist –. It had taken him an hour to get the hint and put his arm around her shoulders. She'd kissed him and he'd been distracted from the film.

She'd told him, before the film, that if she left she couldn't guarantee when or if she could come back.

'You can stay the night then. I know – oh,' he'd blushed. 'I didn't mean like that. You can sleep on the couch. I'll find spare sheets and blankets.'

'I liked that. Jacaranda? What did you think?'

Jacaranda looked up. The closing credits were showing, the lights were coming on and only they were left in the auditorium.

'Yes. I enjoyed it,' she lied effortlessly.

He led her outside and back towards his flat. There were only minor changes to the town she knew: it seemed more studious, grander, the buildings more eloquent of the wealth and prosperity of the city.

'I've an early day tomorrow, Jacaranda, would you like to go out for a meal tomorrow night?'

She nodded. Henghist grinned.

'I'll be quite busy at the library most of the day. Take a look round the city. I'll give you a key to the flat so you can come and go.'

He led the way n, locking the door behind her.

Henghist. I'm not betraying you. How can I? This is an alternate version of you and at least he hasn't lied to me the whole time we've been together.

'If you want to use the bathroom first, I'll wait until you've finished.'

Henghist disappeared up the stairs. There was a stack of sheets, pillows and blankets on the couch.

Jacaranda finished in the bathroom and knocked on Henghist's door.

He took a long time to answer.

'Jacaranda, I don't think we should –'

'Technically we are married.' She lowered her arms, wearing only his boxers. 'Don't I at least get a goodnight kiss?'

He leant over and kissed her cheek. 'Good night, Jacaranda. If you're still sleeping, I'll leave you a note in the morning,' and he gently closed the door on her.

She thought about banging on his door again but rejected it.

He's curious. Where did he separate from the Henghist I thought I knew? She went downstairs. If he'd danced with me all those years ago at the disco. She sighed. I don't know. Who's to say? I was easy, unknowing, and he didn't ask. Will he ever overcome that timidity?

She slept poorly, but at last, with dawn touching the sky, deeply.

Jacaranda woke up at midday, wondering why she was sleeping on a stranger's couch in a stranger's underwear.

Memory returned and she groaned, sitting up, dislodging a note from where it had been placed on the blanket.

'Jacaranda. I've booked us a table at Je t'aime, a French restaurant, for 9 o'clock. They have a strict dress code: you'll need to buy a dress. I've left a card for you to borrow, and directions to a good dress shop and the restaurant. Yours, Henghist.'

Jacaranda shivered. A dress. I don't do dresses.

She showered leisurely, singing poorly at the top of her voice.

Dried off, she scrounged fresh boxers and a T, pulling the jeans Henghist had loaned her back on. She paused in front of the mirror.

'Hmm. Not bad.' She shuddered. 'Good enough for a cheating bastard but is that reason to go to the other extreme?' She touched her cheek. 'Talking to my reflection in a mirror. That's a good sign.'

She shook her head. 'I should just leave. Go home. Leave this Henghist –' she shook her head again. 'He deserves another chance.' She snorted. 'Mind you, short of clambering naked into his bed –' she scowled. 'Henghist, my Henghist, liked me rough and ready. I liked being – like that – for him. But this one.' She shuddered. 'A dress shop? I don't think I've been into one before. He better appreciate it.'

She tucked the flat key, the card, and the note with the card number and the directions on, into her back pocket.

'I've been taken to a dead world. I've done the Roman Empire of the 21st century.' She took a deep breath. 'I can do a dress. It's only a dress shop after all. Nothing to fear.'

--

The sales assistant directed her to the second floor – a personal fitting service, the signs read. Jacaranda fought not to grimace.

'Can I help you, madam?'

She turned. The woman was older than her, though with jet black hair and grey eyes. A harsh face, amplified by the pale orange of her lips.

'I have a date. At a restaurant. Je t'aime.'

The woman raised an eyebrow and took a step back, running her gaze up and down her, tutting, shaking her head.

Jacaranda twisted, feeling like she was in trouble, being reprimanded by someone in authority.

'How long has madam been in the habit of going bra-less?'

'I –'

'And wearing trainers?'

'I –'

'And jeans?'

'I –'

The woman frowned primly. 'I take it you have a strong credit card?'

Jacaranda withdrew Henghist's card.

The woman examined it and nodded. 'I suggest we start with underwear. Take the T shirt off.'

Jacaranda looked around. 'What if someone else comes up?'

The shop floor was about half the size of her retail floor: still large enough for a dozen customers plus husbands, children and sales assistants.

'Then they will see madam being properly measured for a brassiere.'

'I never really –'

The woman sucked her teeth. 'Je t'aime have high standards. Whilst the dresses we sell pass their expectations, they are not intended for –' she paused. 'Immodest women.'

Jacaranda stared. But you would make me – she bit back the comment.

'Fine.' She removed the T and laid it on the counter.

The tape measure was around her before she'd even finished that.

'Lift your arms.'

The tape was pulled tight across her ribs, underneath her breasts. Eased a little. Cold.

'Lower them.'

The sales assistant scratched a note on a pad beside her and crossed to one of the displays.

Jacaranda reached for the T.

'Madam will please leave that. I am attempting to dress you for a prestigious occasion. It is not a place for – T shirts.'

Jacaranda removed her hand.

The hatchet-faced assistant returned with a handful of bras. She took one, lengthened the straps on it. 'Clip it to the first hook and eye.'

'I have worn one before.'

'I find it easiest to assume nothing, madam. To start from scratch.'

Jacaranda clipped it together; pulled the straps up.

'Lean forward into the cups, madam.'

She did as she was ordered. The assistant nodded primly, running fingers over it.

'Flat against the skin at the front. No unsightly bulges.'

Jacaranda bit back her sarcastic comment.

'Straight across the back, straps level and not too tight.'

The assistant stepped back. 'Good. That will do for regular wear. Now. For tonight.'

Jacaranda groaned. 'Won't this do?'

The older woman looked horrified. 'Madam. Please let an artist do her work. You do not have the figure for a V cut – shame, with your height. Therefore it must be off the shoulder. You cannot wear a dress like that and have exposed bra straps. How gauche that would be.'

She drew from the pile the only black bra. 'Strapless and padded for uplift. Now then. Please remove that one.'

An hour, and over two hundred of Henghist's pounds later, the brassiere situation was concluded.

'Now then, madam. Matching underwear. Differing colours is a no-no. The bra being visible beneath the blouse is a no-no.'

'We haven't even got –'

'We will get to the dress later, madam. I need to be assured of each stage. How will you feel if –'

'But it's only a date at a restaurant.'

The sales assistant regarded her coolly. 'Je t'aime is not just a restaurant. It is the place to be seen. And to dine. For a gentleman to take you there he must expect the very highest standards. Anything else would be to let him down. You do not wish to let him down, do you madam?'

Jacaranda shook her head. 'No, miss.'

A slight smile touched the woman's lips. 'Now. What are you going with at the moment?'

She frowned. 'What do you mean?

The woman sighed. 'Underwear, madam. Left to your own devices, what type are you wearing?'

Jacaranda unbuckled the jeans. Eased them down her hips.

'Madam.' The assistant was horrified. 'You are wearing a gentleman's boxers.'

She hung her head. 'They were all he had.'

The woman shook her head. 'And you doubt the need for my instruction? No lady should wear a gentleman's boxers. Ever.'

For twenty minutes she stood cold and naked but for a bra as the assistant had her try on knickers after knickers, trying different styles, looking for the perfect match for the white daily and the black special occasions' bra.

'Finally.'

The assistant nodded. 'Next we have the hose.'

Jacaranda groaned.

Three hours later the assistant drew aside the curtain on a wall to reveal a full-length mirror.

'Now, madam. What do you say?'

Jacaranda stared. The hair was still hers, faded at the ends where she'd used to dye it regularly. The face was still her: thin, pale lips, glittering blue eyes. But the body, the dress –

The neck was swan like, though she could still see the faint marks on her throat, bruises from the previous morning's struggle. The shoulders were pale and creamy, rarely so exposed.

The dress was black and figure-clinging, not that she'd have said she had a figure, but the strapless bra had given her definition. It made her feel horribly exposed.

Everybody notices my eyes – or my nose – first. With this – she tried not to shudder. I feel like I'm exposing myself. Putting my breasts on display when it's mostly padding.

She lifted her hand. The sales assistant knocked it aside.

'Don't reveal you are unused to this. The gentleman may have met you when you dressed like something from the slums, but you are a lady.'

Jacaranda scowled, fed up with the whole thing and regretting it. 'And ladies go round saying "look at my chest, not my face, because Heaven forbid you might find personality and intelligence in my face".'

The older woman sighed. 'I can give you the appearance of a lady, only. When you open your mouth, it is obvious –'

She looked away. The dress ended mid-thigh. Even with black hose her legs felt too long, too awkward, too exposed.

'Now then, I cannot do anything about your diction –'

'My diction is just fine. In fact –'

'In fact, madam, the job is poorly done if you abandon the attempt now. The dress and the underwear is perfect, but there remains the matter of the shoes.'

'Shoes?'

She nodded. 'Heels, naturally, although not large ones. And finally hair, nails and make up.'

Jacaranda groaned.

At quarter past nine she tottered into Je t'aime. The heels were low but pinched her toes. Her hair had been rinsed, treated and teased, tweaked into something between curls and spikes. Pale blue eye shadow had been applied. They'd applied foundation to her cheeks, and to her throat, to hide the bruises.

They'd tried a dozen shades of lipstick, eventually choosing a pale lilac shade.

'Your colouring is unfortunately rather gothic, madam. Too pale skin. Dark hair. So we have accentuated your eyes and hence must also amplify your lips.'

The maitre d' ushered her to her chair.

'The gentleman has confirmed he will be late, and asked us to take a drink's order off you.'

Jacaranda ordered champagne and the maitre d' scuttled off gleefully.

She looked around, trying not to catch anyone's eyes. Am I mutton dressed as lamb or do I look alright? The dress had ridden up and she didn't want to cross her legs but could feel a cold draft.

Henghist. I wasn't even this tarted up for our wedding.

She sighed. The wedding you told me we were having. All my life I did what you said. What you suggested. You were my sun, my moon. She scowled. My lord and master. I knew no better.

Jacaranda closed her eyes. There were too many memories of sex and not many of them just talking. I meet an alternate Henghist and the first thing on my mind is getting into bed with him. She groaned.

'Are you okay, madam?'

The maitre d' had returned with the champagne: poured her a glass.

She took it automatically. 'Yes. I'm fine.' She paused. 'Actually, no I'm not. I'm really not alright.'

'This is possibly not the place you should be then, madam,' he answered blandly.

'My husband of twenty-five years spent our marriage lying to me and tried to get me killed. I'm here with another man and all I can think about is seducing him. I've spent nine hours, nine hours,' she repeated, getting to her feet, 'getting ready for this date and I'm feeling uncomfortable because I feel like I'm on display. I look beautiful and it makes me uncomfortable because I don't know how to deal with it. Nobody's ever told me how to deal with those things.'

'Madam, we really,' the maitre d' began.

'I'm not going to cause a scene in your prestigious restaurant. Here, take this,' and she dropped Henghist's credit card on the table. 'Tell him I'm sorry, but it's too late.'

She stalked out into the night. Tried to; her ankle almost gave way and she kicked the heels off.

It was similar to her Reading. She found the shopping centre and sat on the bank of the canal. The water was black and limpid, unhastening. The tears flowed down her cheeks.

Sometime later she became aware of someone close by.

'It's never too late, Jacaranda.'

She turned. Henghist – Curator Goring – put his jacket around her shoulders.

'You're freezing. And beautiful.'

Jacaranda sniffed back a sob. 'My eye shadow's run, I've lost my shoes and the hose is full of ladders –'

He laughed, and hugged her, and kissed her cheek. 'If I thought it was too late, I'd never have asked you to the pictures.'

'I'm glad you did.'

'Even if you didn't enjoy it.'

She began to protest but he shook his head gently. 'It doesn't matter. I'm glad I asked you to the restaurant though.'

'Glad?' She sniffed. 'You haven't seen what all this cost yet –'

He leant in and kissed her nose. 'It was worth it. Even if,' he coughed.

'If?' she asked.

He chuckled. 'Even if my memories of last night seem to suggest –'

Jacaranda smiled, running her hands over her chest. 'The wonders of an uplift bra.'

Henghist smiled. 'You came on strong. I almost didn't show at all tonight.'

Jacaranda nodded. 'I know. I'm glad you did though. That place was a bit – swanky.'

He shrugged. 'I was trying to show off. The maitre d' – and several customers – repeated your speech to me. Word for word.'

She looked away.

He slipped his arm round her shoulders.

Jacaranda nestled in to him.

He let his hand slide down to cup her breast.

'Henghist –' she said softly.

'I know you're married and I know this is – wrong, I supposed, but I get the feeling –'

She stopped him with a kiss.

'When I leave here, I'm going home to regain my life and take what's mine. I have a score to settle with the Henghist who married me so he could control the gateway. I don't know how it works or if I can or will be able to come back this way again.'

She could feel him pulling away from her emotionally if not physically.

'But I think, if you'd kissed me at the disco, things would have been different.' She kissed him again. 'I would like them to have been different, but they are the way they are.'

He nodded slowly. 'I know.'

'That doesn't mean you won't find somebody,' and she smiled, putting her hand over his, 'who'll do more than let you feel her up and kiss her.'

She kissed him gently, softly.

'Goodbye, Henghist.'

She broke the kiss. Turned away and got to her feet before he could see her tears.

The Unforsaken Land

He was standing on the beach.

'How did I –'

The sea rolled upon the shore, more green than blue, but maybe sea was wrong. He could see a landmass in the distance, rising but low, but dark and somehow threatening.

The water flowed more like a river now, passing the bank where he stood –

The bank where previously it had been a beach.

Seaweed grew in the water, trailing veins that brushed the beach; that brushed the bank.

Miles closed his eyes, remembering his name, remembering –

'I was not – what?'

The faintest of breezes blew, but it came from behind him, out to the sea or the river. He turned.

The grassy bank was a sandy beach. He blinked. The bank remained a beach, one overlaid upon the other.

'New, huh?'

Miles looked up. He'd noticed the mist earlier; seen it before he'd remembered who he was. But one patch of mist had solidified.

'The name's Louise. You'll get used to it.'

Louise was dressed like a goth, except they probably called themselves emo now. Long, battered coat, going threadbare. Woolly jumper and too large jeans. Buttons on the jacket, bands he recognised. Her hair was white, kind of Cruella de ville, but with a single swathe of black.

She touched her hair automatically. 'My mother always hated my hair. It's a small price to pay though.'

Miles frowned. 'What the hell is going on?'

Louise shook her head. 'You're new. Dead but not dead. Not yet.'

'Are you –'

She laughed, a slightly rusty sound. 'I'm not a guardian angel or anything naff like that. I'm dead, like you.'

Miles blinked. 'I'm sorry? What the fu –'

Louise sighed. 'You are dead. Deceased. Departed. Done for.'

She shivered, shaking her head. 'I'm sorry. It's hard to get used to. Hard, living through a veil.'

Miles rubbed his brow. The low landmass caught his gaze. It certainly wasn't Margate, but anything else –

'That's the Forgotten Land.'

He turned to look at Louise. Her hair was black, with a streak of white. Her face was puffy, bruised. She wore fingerless gloves: her hands shook with the cold.

He blinked. Her hair was white. There was a bit more colour in her cheeks. The harshness was gone from her face; she looked more alive.

Louise frowned. 'You're seeing me as – she – sees – saw – me, aren't you?'

Miles shook his head. 'I have no idea what the hell is going on –'

'This is the Unforsaken Land.'

Her voice was cold and small, timid, cowering. He suspected if he looked her hair would be black.

'We're dead but remembered. What we are here,' her voice grew warmer, thicker. 'Is who we are as we are remembered.'

Miles glanced at Louise. Her eyes were a vivid, pale blue. 'What happened to you?'

She looked away. 'I was a teenage girl. I committed suicide.' She shrugged. 'Hormones.'

Miles looked away. The ocean sea river was no more decided on its state than it had been.

'He abused me. My stepfather. She believed him.' Her voice was harsh, brittle, terrible in its bleakness. 'I ran away. It was no better. Drugs. Sex.' She shivered. 'Cold. Always cold. Stealing. Living in a squat.'

'I was a princess when I was younger. There'd be a man. A husband. A house in the country. Roses round the door. Three point six kids for my mother to babysit –'

Mist drifted over the water. If he concentrated he could just see living shadows within the mist as it was drawn across the water to the black isle.

'That would be a merciful release. This.' Louise screamed.

Miles turned. Louise's hair colour was changing strand by strand, blurring so fast, until it looked alive.

'What – what's going on?'

She screamed again, and her hair darkened. 'Bitch. You betrayed me. You were supposed to love me but you didn't believe me. You were useless. Useless. USELESS. Fucking useless.'

Miles caught her arm and she half turned. Her eyes were dark, bloodshot, large in her colourless face. 'She's thinking happy thoughts about me and I'm dead and trapped here and this is closer to who I was –'

She half shuddered, shaking her head and moving back, her hair fading to white.

'Just a teenage girl. So stupid. I told –' she ground her teeth together, fighting.

'I. Didn't. Fucking. Lie.' She hissed through clenched teeth. 'Cal liked that I was scared of him. That I was innocent. He liked it and she didn't believe me and it was no better when I ran away –' she paused, calming, taking a breath.

'It's not always this bad.' She almost smiled. 'You're not conflicted. You're lucky. Mommy dearest just wouldn't believe – couldn't believe – that her new man could – would – do such things.'

She took his hand and squeezed it. 'How did you get here?' She released his hand.

Miles shook his head. 'I was – in a church. Admiring the stained glass. There was a priest.' He shrugged. 'I thought he was a priest. He had a trilby. A long leather coat.' He grimaced. 'Like no priest I'd ever seen.'

'Priests.' Louise spat, her dark hair flying. 'He came round for tea and sat there not saying a word. He didn't believe me either. Bastard.'

'I never wanted to be a nun when I was younger. I always wanted a man. A husband. I'd have taken my kids and –'

Louise cursed and spat.

'Bastard. Bastard. Bastard. I hate this. I wish I was dead and forgotten. I want the Forgotten Land. I don't want this. Half me, half her remembered version of me.'

She fell to her knees, pounding the beach, the grassy slope.

'There's got to be a way out of here.'

Louise looked up at him. Tears blotched her cheeks. She sniffed, wiping her nose on the back of her hand.

'We're dead.'

He nodded slowly. 'Yes. But nobody knows. Nobody told us of this.' He offered her his hand. 'Come on.'

Louise frowned.

'You can fight to be who you are, not who others remember you as, right?'

She nodded slowly.

'Then why can't we fight this? Why just accept it? There's got to be a way back, a way out.'

Miles knew then that the priest had murdered him. That the priest wasn't a priest, that he wasn't murdered for or because of who he was, but because of who and what he worked for.

The bookshop, he thought, with growing dread. If the assassin goes after Jacaranda –

I have no family. No partner. The only one who'll remember me is her. If she dies –

He drew Louise up slowly. Her hair was more black than white.

'Come on. There's got to be a way out. A way through.'

'What's the point?' Louise protested.

He smiled grimly. 'We won't know until we try. Or do you want to stay here, like this? Do you want your mother's version to be the right one?'

Louise's hair went black. Her lips went pale, her eyes dark.

'If I can get that bastard back –'

'If we can get them back –'

Louise looked at him and grinned, madness and passion in her cobalt blue eyes.

Veil of Tears

'If you will take my hand –'

The woman sat back hastily, snatching her hand away, clutching her handbag compulsively. 'I. I don't like,' she lowered her eyes. 'I have a skin disorder.'

Bridge sat back. Eliza – Liz to her friends – her client, perched uneasily on the edge of a chair. There probably wasn't much difference in age, though worry lines etched Liz's face. There was a touch of white in her hair, and her clothes, though respectable, were of someone older.

'If you want my help –'

'I do.' Eliza's head snapped up. 'I mean. I heard. You are a medium, aren't you?' She fumbled with the clasps of her handbag. 'I brought some of Josie's things. That's what –'

'Eliza.' Bridge shook her head. 'I am not a medium. I am a grief counsellor.'

'They said,' Eliza sniffed. 'They said you were. You'd need –'

'Who said?' Bridge asked, leaning back in her chair. The eye of a digital recorder winked at her unobtrusively from the bookshelf.

Eliza blew her nose, tucking the tissue into her sleeve. The blouse was too severe, too plain, too formal. It didn't sit right with the small gold ring on the littlest finger of Eliza's right hand.

'I brought some of her toys. That's what you do, don't you? I've seen it in the movies. You touch –'

Bridge eased a shoe off, rubbing the heel of one foot against the other. 'If. If I'm able to find anything,' she stressed, 'it'll only prove that –' she glanced at her notes, 'that Josephine,' she trailed off.

Eliza nodded. 'I know. I want to know – I need to know. One way or the other. I can pay. Whatever you charge by the hour.'

Bridge frowned. 'I do not do séances, Miss Jones.' She shook her head. 'No Ouija boards. No candles, no voices from the ether.'

Eliza looked at her in genuine surprise. 'Then how do –'

Bridge gave her a tight smile. 'It can take a week or so. Sometimes,' she shrugged. 'Sometimes there is nothing I can do for a client. No message I can relay. I guarantee no success.'

Eliza looked disappointed. 'If it's money –'

Bridge shook her head. 'Money is nothing to the spirits of the departed. Some want to talk. Some have nothing to say. Some,' she shrugged.

Eliza was frowning. 'A week?' Her frown deepened. 'A week so you can investigate me. So you find out – all about me.' A warning gleam appeared in her eye.

Bridge forced herself to relax. 'You can walk away now, Liz, and never know. I'm not forcing you to do anything.'

Liz sat on the edge of the chair, frozen, uncertain. Bridge let her gaze drift away, lose focus. Eliza was her first client since – she shuddered. DI Gray had made a big deal of finding James Corcoran in her office. That very chair she thought, glancing back at Liz.

'I'll do it,' the woman said in a low voice, 'but not a week. Now. Tell me what you can find out about my Josie.'

Bridge shrugged. 'You want me to look for your daughter's spirit? You want me to tell you if she's dead.'

Eliza looked down for a moment, as if noticing something on the carpet, then looked up and nodded. 'Yes. Tell me about –' she paused, looking away again, 'my daughter.'

Bridge stood up. She closed the curtains behind her, shutting out the cold grey world.

'Wh – why are you doing that?' Liz stammered.

She turned back to face her client. 'Do you want to see – what I see? Do you want to meet Josephine – face to face?'

Eliza stared at her, getting up from the chair and backing away. 'He didn't – they didn't –' she amended hastily.

Bridge closed the distance between them. 'You've nothing to be afraid of.' She smiled. 'Really.'

She reached out and caught Liz's hand. The woman tried to pull away but Bridge held her fast. 'Who sent you?' she asked, feeling the room grow colder, darker, feeling the bridge form beneath her. 'Who orchestrated this charade, Liz? There is no Josephine.'

Infinite night blossomed above her. No clouds. No stars. Liz whimpered.

'Where are we? What is – how?'

Bridge laughed, releasing the other woman's hand. 'This is the bridge. It has no other name.' She looked at the other woman coldly. 'I discovered it when I was eleven. Eleven.' She shook her head. 'The age you said Josephine was. But there is no Josephine, is there?'

She raised the woman's chin with her finger. 'Who, exactly, are you?'

Liz's teeth were chattering. 'Get me – get me out of here. Please.'

Bridge shook her head. 'This is the bridge. Whether it's between life and death, or between ourselves and our conscience, I don't know.' She smiled. 'But it looks like someone knows you.'

A pastel shape was forming out of the darkness that marked both ends of the bridge, approaching with slow, tottering, childlike steps.

Liz turned and looked; grabbed her and pushed her in front. 'No. No. Make it go away. Make it stop. It didn't – I didn't – I was only –'

The shape came closer: a child, no more than a couple of years old. She smiled as the soul of the infant approached, shaking loose Liz's terrified hands, and knelt down.

'Hello. My name's Bridge.'

The pastel shape of the child looked at her. She could almost make out the features, the baby-blonde hair, the chubby cheeks and golden curls.

'Liz. Liza,' the spirit called.

Bridge smiled, sensing Eliza freeze behind her.

'No. No. I didn't mean – I was only young – I didn't mean –'

The child looked up at her. 'I know you.'

Bridge stared, feeling her blood thicken and slow. 'What? How?'

'You are the keeper,' the child continued in a singsong voice. 'The gatekeeper. The gatekeeper of the bridge. I wanted to meet you. I've waited so long to meet you.'

'Eliza,' Bridge hissed, 'now would be a good time to explain.'

There was no reply. She glanced over her shoulder. Eliza was on her knees, head in her hands.

'Don't cry,' said the child, moving past her.

Bridge moved back, unwilling to let the shade touch or come too near her.

Liz looked up, rocking back onto her heels. 'I didn't mean to do it. I was only a child.'

'I know,' the pastel shade said, slivers of light stroking the woman's cheek. 'I know you didn't mean it. I'm having fun here. There's plenty of people to play with. I am never alone. Not like you.'

Eliza was crying, her body racking with sobs. The shade was half curled around her, spectral face to tear-blotched face, and Bridge suddenly saw the resemblance.

'Your sister. This is your sister.'

Liz wiped her eyes, her arm half around the wraith-like child that was her sister's soul. 'I. I was only four or five. Mum and dad had had another baby.' She looked shyly at her sibling. 'I was jealous. I tried not to be for so long.' She frowned. 'I thought my parents would get rid of me in favour of – in favour of –' she broke off again, crying anew.

The spirit child consoled her elder sibling.

Bridge looked away. She had regained much, but there was one thing she never could. One thing that drew her back to the bridge regardless of the pain it caused.

The spirit of the child looked up at her. 'You are the gatekeeper. You are not alone.'

Bridge stared. 'What do you me –'

'There are others like you.' The child continued consoling her grieving client. 'Other bridges. Other –' the shade paused. 'Other junctions.' She smiled. 'Other meeting spots.'

Bridge shook her head. 'Do you know – how?' she asked breathlessly. 'Why?'

The shade shook her head. 'We do not know. What is this place to us? Occasionally one of us is drawn to a bridge. While we are remembered we remain. I have waited so long.' She stroked Eliza's hair tenderly. 'My big sister sent me here. She didn't know what she was doing. I am grateful.'

Bridge stared. 'Grateful? Your sister – Eliza – murdered you.'

The shade gave a nonchalant shrug. 'There is no pain here. No tiredness. No bed time.' She smiled up at Bridge. 'No hurt. I can see you are hurt. Won't you join us? It won't hurt.'

Bridge stared. The temptation to end it. The call of the bottle or the pills. To lose control of the car. Or, simply, to stop. To remain on the bridge. To deny the world out there. The world that had light, and hurt, and pain, and addiction, and –

'There is someone waiting for you,' the spirit said softly.

Bridge backed away. 'I promised. My mentor. I betrayed him. He cannot. If I stay –' she turned to run, to flee. He had me in life. He won't have me in death.

'Your daughter.'

The words tore at her ears; rent her heart. Samantha. She choked back a sob. I always look for her. I have never – she turned back to the shade of Eliza's sister. 'Is she here? Is my Samantha here? Can I see her? Just once. That's all I crave. My little girl –'

The shade shook her head. 'If you stay, you can journey on with her. But if you return to your world, she will not come.'

Bridge frowned. 'Why not? Every time I come to this place I look for her. You came when I brought your sister. Why doesn't Samantha come to me?' She choked back her grief. 'Does she hate me? Because she went on. I survived. I didn't want to. I wanted to –'

'She cannot come to you. You should go. Take my sister with you.'

Eliza raised her head. 'Do you forgive me? I – I was only a child.'

The shade nodded. 'Of course I do. Live happy; do not forget me.'

Bridge could almost see the spirit slipping away. Could feel the nausea rising that always came when she spent too long on the bridge.

'Come on.' Eliza was standing, brushing dirt from her skirt, nose wrinkled as if she'd smelt something bad. 'We should go.'

Bridge watched as the pastel dissolved into the darkness that perpetually shrouded the bridge. What did it say? While we are remembered we remain. Samantha, she thought. I will find you. I will get in contact with you.

'Come on,' said Eliza briskly. 'We should – I need you to – do whatever you do. Get us – out of here.'

Bridge saw the tightness in her knuckles. So close to breaking, she thought. Still, if she wants to fool herself.

The transition wasn't easy. Somewhere in the darkness is Samantha. Why doesn't she come to me? What's holding her back?

'That's better.' Eliza shook her head. 'I must have been –
'

Bridge became aware she was back in her office; Eliza was standing by the door, wanting to go but hesitant.

'Who are you?'

Eliza pursed her lips. 'I was undercover. I never expected –' she shuddered.

Bridge rubbed her brows. I need to lie down in a darkened room until the world stops spinning. Or have a drink to spin it the other way.

'Your boss?'

The light, pale as it was, was making her eyes hurt. Unconsciousness was sliding up on her.

Eliza scowled. 'DI Gray. He wanted to know more about you. When Corcoran was found in your office, and he was linked to –'

Samantha, she thought as tiredness overcame her. I will find you. Even if I have to stay on the bridge, I will find you.

Ghosts in the machine

Cliveden led the way. It wasn't just that he was a year older – Staples' mother had told her firmly that girls were every bit as good as boys.

'You'll see,' her mother had said the last time she'd given her the speech, her arms covered in flour from baking to celebrate her father's expected return home, 'what with the war – I mean the Incident With Germany, they'll need girls to do the jobs of men. Don't let anyone tell you –'

Staples knew all about the War with Germany: only her mother insisted on calling it the Incident. They'd moved out of London to avoid the worst of it, but she missed it. Reading wasn't much fun.

She'd become friends with Cliveden by chance. He was a local boy who looked down on London and always said he'd never leave his home town no matter what. He'd been quite snobby about it. But one day she'd found him crying and he'd admitted his mother was taking him away, taking him south, to the coast, to escape the expected bombing of Reading.

He'd looked so lonely and scared – and Staples remembered how she'd felt on being told they were leaving London – that she spoke to her mother and her mother spoke to his and suddenly he was staying with them, even though his own mother had gone south.

She'd had lots of friends in London, and many of them were children of men fighting in the war, but a couple weren't, and Staples suspected she actually knew more about the war than her mother would, though it would have been rude to say so.

But Cliveden was her first friend in Reading and, once he'd got over being snobby and superior, he was actually a good chum. He'd taken her to a nice spot by the river, where they'd tried to fish and had shared the half rotten apple he'd saved especially for her. He'd shown her which abandoned houses were safe to play in and which weren't, and taught her which ARP wardens to avoid and which, with a bit of play acting and looking downcast, might give them a biscuit or a stale piece of bread (which he shared with her, after they became friends, if she wasn't with him).

And then, after they'd been friends about six months, he'd let her into his biggest secret.

'I've got this place, Staples. If my mother is acting strange – like if there's an uncle in the house, I'll go there. Always at night. It's safe there. There's no one else there, and it's warm, and nobody knows about it. Nobody but you now.'

She hadn't said anything at first. It was his big secret and his face was glistening with sweat. She wasn't entirely sure he wasn't imagining it. She knew what his mother and his uncles were up to – that'd be enough to make anyone leave their house.

'Even if bombs are falling,' one of her friends in London had boasted, 'I'd rather the bombs than hearing my mum –' he'd broken off, crimson-faced, embarrassed.

'There's lots of books to read, and you can sleep in peace and quiet. If the bombs ever fall, I know where to hide,' and he jabbed his thumb against his chest, 'I know where to hide.'

It was his secret – if it was a real place – and so she'd let him lead the way.

He'd led the way out of the house and through the deserted, darkened town, finding his way, often by touch, dodging the ARP wardens that hunted for any light that might draw a stray German plane in to bomb them.

He tried the handle of a shop.

'Cliveden, we can't –'

A faint light gleamed within as the door opened. He darted in and she followed.

'If we get caught –'

He shushed her, rummaging through his pockets for a piece of wire. He slipped it into the lock and began waggling it about.

He pulled back after a couple of minutes.

'It's locked,' Staples said, 'we shouldn't be –'

Cliveden shook his head, grinned, and pushed the door open.

Staples felt her breath catch in her throat. There was a large room inside, with lots of brightly coloured things on the shelves – shelves and shelves of them. Whosoever's shop it was was hoarding –

She entered the room and wrinkled her nose. It smelt of dust, and something acidic, like lemon, not that the greengrocers had seen a lemon for years, let alone sold one.

They were books, she realised, on the shelves, but not the plain coloured types she'd expected, not common missals and a child's guide to nature. The covers were made of paper. Unrationed paper – not that she was sure why paper was rationed.

There was a table in front of her with a book of pictures of art in it. Cliveden was turning the pages idly. He stopped, his breath cut off. He was looking at a picture of a painting of a lady with no clothes on.

'Why does she look like that?' he asked, turning to her.

Staples looked past him. It was a shop, but not like any she'd known. If people knew how much paper was here, they'd stampede it, she thought. No making do for the loo or for fire lighting.

The books are wrong. They're too openly displayed. Anyone could steal one and they'd never know. The shop's too big for such a small thing – where would the shopkeeper stand?

Her eyes were drawn to a higher table with displays and a machine on it and behind that table –

'Good evening,' said the woman, and she looked like she'd only just woken up, 'should you be here?'

Cliveden turned and yelped, knocking the book he'd been staring at off the table and heading for the door.

The woman laughed. She wasn't a traditional beauty, Staples thought. Her nose was a bit too long, and her hair was cut in a very strange style and appeared to be different colours.

'There's no need to run. My name is Jacaranda Rhoad. What are yours?'

Staples caught at Cliveden and stopped him running out on her. 'Pick the book up,' she hissed. 'My name is Staples, m'am. Sarah Tarples. Everyone calls me Staples.'

The woman smiled. Staples thought she knew all the shopkeepers in the small town, but she didn't recognise the woman or her shop.

'You can call me Jacaranda. What about your friend?'

Cliveden looked up, embarrassed. He couldn't get the book back onto the display stand: had laid it face down, then saw the back cover painting and didn't know where to look.

Staples elbowed him.

He looked up at the woman. 'My name is Eustace Edward Diggory Montgomery Cliveden. Everyone just calls me Cliveden.' He frowned a little. 'My mother thought giving me lots of names would do me good. Please miss, we didn't mean any harm.'

The woman smiled again. 'Well, you woke me up, but that's no bad thing. It's late at night though – don't you have homes to go to?'

Staples nodded. 'Yes, m'am. We live at –' she glanced at Cliveden. 'Cliveden's living with us because his mother was afraid the Germans would bomb Reading. My mum moved out of London to avoid bombs.'

She smiled sympathetically. 'Was it bad in London?'

Staples sighed. 'There were lots of broken houses to play in. And mates –' she looked at Cliveden, 'I mean I was part of a gang there. There's just Cliveden and I –'

'I found this place.' Cliveden looked up, lifting his chin. 'I wanted somewhere – a bit – peaceful. I would come here and read in the dark.' He swallowed. 'I hope I didn't –'

A look of understanding crossed her face. 'I thought, occasionally, that things weren't quite as I left them. Is the war bad?'

Cliveden's face darkened. She didn't think he was going to answer, but he surprised her.

'Mum was glad when dad went to war. I miss him. She has uncles round, and sometimes they bring me things, but I miss my dad.' He sighed. 'Mum didn't want to risk the bombs and left. Staples' mum took me in, gave me a home.' He smiled, more confident. 'Staples' a good friend. For a girl,' he added as an afterthought.

'Well,' and the woman smiled warmly, hand in her hair, 'any time you want to –'

'Here. What's going on –'

Staples whirled. One of the ARP wardens was standing in the doorway. His speechless gaze took in the shelves of books.

'You've been hoarding.' He frowned. 'This looks like imported stuff. You'll have to come with me.'

He broke off, looking at the book that had embarrassed Cliveden. 'Nuddy books as well. You've got a lot of explaining to do. And with kids in the shop as well. Shame on you – where's your war spirit?' he frowned. 'You one of those liberal types who doesn't believe in war? Your husband a coward?'

The woman came from behind the table and Staples could see she was angry.

'Trousers and all.' The warden looked even more hostile. 'You one of those women? Like young girls, do you? Your kind should be shot. You're disgusting. Perverted. Corrupting young minds –'

'I am not a pervert,' and Staples remembered the woman had said her name was Jacaranda. It sounded Yank. It definitely wasn't British.

'Do you like being a warden because you can bully people? Or do you like it because it gives you the right to try to get into houses?'

'Now see here –' the warden drew himself up.

Staples tried not to laugh. The warden was fat, even with the two years of rationing, and wasn't even close to being as tall as Jacaranda.

Staples realised the woman was beautiful and mysterious and a little bit frightening but, despite all that, she trusted her. She liked her.

'I think you should go, warden. Before you say anything you really will come to regret. You won't have any cause to come in here again.'

He looked ready for a fight but Jacaranda stood her ground, unafraid of him. Once or twice his fists clenched, as if he'd hit her, but then he wheeled about and strode out.

Jacaranda let out a sigh of relief.

'I thought he was going to hit you,' Staples said.

Jacaranda smiled at her. 'So did I. Cliveden, can you check the front door is properly shut please. I don't want him returning. Then I'll see what biscuits I've got.'

Cliveden went out and closed the front door.

Staples asked quietly. 'What did he mean – one of those women?'

Jacaranda smiled and shook her head. 'I don't think I should tell you. But I was married for twenty-five years.'

'Is that the latest fashion?' Cliveden asked. 'Women wearing trousers?'

'Of course it is,' Staples answered, 'it's come over from the States. Everyone knows that.'

Jacaranda laughed. 'Make yourselves comfortable.' She yawned. 'I'll go and get you some biscuits.' Her laugh faded and she looked from one to the other. 'You are welcome to come here any night when you want a safe place. But you must close the front door, and you must check who's in here, in case there's anybody else in. Do you understand?'

She nodded. Cliveden nodded.

Jacaranda's smile brightened her face. 'Right then. Stay here, I'll fetch us all some biscuits and tea. Maybe a little cheese. We can have a wartime midnight snack.'

Cliveden's belly rumbled. She smiled and Jacaranda laughed but Cliveden just looked embarrassed.

'Don't worry.' Staples patted his hand. 'I'll look after you.'

Eve white / Eve black

'I don't know why I put up with you, Kevin. This is really not good enough a report. On the first page alone, I found twenty-seven errors. I could go through it page by page – error by error – but I'm not sure you'd learn. I'll have to work late to redo it all. Get out of my sight. I don't want to see or think of you 'til Monday – at least.'

He backed out of her office, giving her his best cute-pathetic look. Like I'd fall for a loser like that. Eve scowled. Some silly bitch did. Left him with a mortgage he can't afford and a bloody sprog. And he always wants time off to look after it. Aren't there kennels or convent schools or places he could send it to?

She waited until the door was closed and she'd heard his bumbling footsteps retreating, his murmured goodbye to Annie, her PA, before retrieving the offending report.

Eve flicked through it idly. It was an amazing document. Kevin the klutz had such good foresight and didn't realise it. Still probably desperately hoping for a smile from her. She grinned. If the management board go through with its proposals – her smile broadened. I'll arrange for Kevin to win the office lottery. A long weekend for one in some leisure resort. It'll screw him up. Take a holiday or look after kiddie. He'll have no choice but to turn it down.

The intercom buzzed.

'Have you any more work for me, Ms Lawson?'

Eve glanced at the clock. Her PA was insufferably competent and unattractively fertile. Annie had three grown sons and a much younger daughter. She knew Annie was subtler – and cleverer – than Kevin in many ways, but lacking that something that he had. Eve suspected Annie could do her job; suspected she'd reward Kevin rather than keep him down.

155

'You can go, Annie. I've got work to do.'

She sat poring over the report until the light in the outer room went out. Annie would be long gone, rushing home to her claustrophying family.

Eve closed the report. Kevin had done his job; she only had to alter the odd line or figure and it would guarantee her success.

The office at night was her freedom. She had master keys for all the cabinets and drawers. It was easy enough for things to be lost, stolen, misplaced. It kept her staff on their toes. But tonight she felt like doing something different. Something greater.

--

'I don't know why you haven't risen further, Kevin. This is a really excellent report. I went through it line by line and I couldn't find a single flaw, and I know you've got other things on your mind.'

Eve could hear the smile in Annie's voice as her boss continued.

'Take Monday off. Spend some time with that daughter of yours.'

Eve flicked the intercom off as Kevin came out, smiling with relief.

'Night, Kevin.'

He stopped and flashed her a smile. He was fat and balding, harried-looking and a single parent. He wiped his brow.

'Good night, Eve. Have a good weekend.'

Kevin was hardly out of the room than Annie's door opened and her boss came out.

'C'mon, Eve. Friday night. You must have a partner somewhere. Or a bar calling your name.'

Eve smiled back at Annie. The mother of four was an excellent boss, the best she'd ever worked for.

'Well, I was going to go to the bookshop.'

Annie shook her head good naturedly. 'There's more to life than reading about it. Get out there. Do something exciting.' She smiled. 'Wake up on Monday morning in someone else's bed with no idea how you got there.'

Eve couldn't help but blush. Annie waved her farewell, still smiling. Eve finished off her work, tidying her desk and closing the computer down.

She glanced up at the shut door, at the darkened office beyond. 'But I do intend to do something this weekend.'

--

It was easy enough to crack the passwords on Kevin's computer. Every one was his daughter's name. Annie's weren't that much more difficult: her sons and her daughter's names.

Hiding the hardcore images took longer: Annie regularly checked her system.

'I'll have Annie's randomly chosen and dumped for security checking.' She glanced at some of the images and smirked. 'Having those found on her system will take her down a peg or two.'

Using Kevin's logon details she signed up to several X-rated and cross-dressing sites. She sniggered at the thought of the ill-favoured klutz getting explicit videos on his work account.

She closed both computers down. I'll change what I need on Kevin's report then –

A sound made her look up. The main office door was closing.

'Who's there?'

Eve strode down the office to it. I locked it. I know I did.

The door opened to her touch. There was nobody in the corridor beyond. The lifts were locked down. Both loos were empty.

'I must have imagined it.'

She went back through the office. It didn't seem so open, so free, as it once had. Eve shook her head. I'm working too hard. It wouldn't be good for anyone if I was ill. They wouldn't be able –

'Hello.'

Eve yelped in surprise. Stared. Screamed. Then *she* was moving and before she could react, she was falling and –

--

Eve stared at her handiwork. The other Eve was tied to the computer chair, arms bound behind her back and gagged.

She leant in and slapped her other self.

Eve's eyes flew open and she tried to move: the chair rolled sideways.

Eve grinned. 'You've probably got lots of questions, sister, but don't worry about it. So have I, but I know I'm not clever enough to answer them.'

The other Eve was staring at her in horror, shock, disbelief.

Eve chuckled. 'I've been watching you. The alternate me.' She shook her head. 'It's never your fault. You never take responsibility, only credit.'

She paced around behind her other self. Spun her a few times before relenting.

'It always bugged me, people like you. They would take credit for what others did. They never seemed to fail. I did a good job, but never got the recognition.' She shrugged, grinning. 'You'd probably say I lacked the killer instinct. I just never got why my ascent should be at someone else's expense.'

She moved away again, to the other side of Eve's desk.

'Then I found this aberration. A hole in reality, or a gateway, or a portal or something. And do you know what I found?'

She – the other Eve, the Eve of this reality – stared.

'Lost for words? How unlike me. I found you. A self centred careerist. You trample everyone before you. You'd die alone and unloved but for one thing.'

Eve was trying to speak, muffled by the gag.

'You're really not me, you know. I'm – calm. Mostly. Thoughtful. I wonder where the difference began.' She smiled at her alternate self. 'Were you denied a Barbie when you were younger – or something equally meaningless – or were you born a thoughtless bitch?'

Eve growled at her, fury in her eyes now. Eve grinned. 'Come on. We're going for a walk.'

She pushed her alternate self out of her office – Eve shook her head. In my world this is Annie's office – and into the general office.

'I'm afraid using the lifts is a no-no. You've a choice, me, dearest. Will I push you down the stairs or will you behave?'

--

Eve let the fake untie her without fuss. The other woman – the spineless one – retied her ankles so she could only shuffle.

Kevin must have put this woman up to it. Or Annie. I'll give you she's almost the spit of me, but so moderate. Soft.

The other woman pushed her. 'Go down to the car park. If you try anything, I've got the rope that's tied to your ankles. I'd rather not have you bloodied in here, but I can always clean it up later.'

Eve began shuffling down carefully. Her arms ached but the knots actually felt looser. She tied me around the chair. Now that's gone I've more flexibility. The gag I can bite through. She almost smirked. The silly bitch should have used a ball gag.

She descended the levels slowly. The guard's gone. The car park is just ours. If she thinks she's going to best me with her touchy-feely ways –

The stairs ended and she stopped opposite the basement door.

'Move back. Let me open it.'

Eve shuffled back. The other Eve still held the rope tightly. The imposter keyed in the code and the door slid open –

Eve dropped to her knees, pulling her ankles back. The other woman spun, pulled off balance and fell. Eve fell on top of her, slamming her head repeatedly against her attacker's. As the pain exploded, the other woman went limp.

--

There was pain. Pain like she'd never felt before. The taste – she knew it instinctively – of blood on her lips. She could feel it, congealed on her face. A cut above her right eye.

Her wrists, her ankles, ached. Rope, pulled tight. Something hard and large that she was tied to.

'Is my dear self awake yet?'

She opened her eyes. Tried to. Her right refused to cooperate.

She was in the underground car park, tied to a pillar. The other Eve, the credit-taking Eve, was there. Her car stood a few metres away, door open, engine running.

'I just have to reverse – all an accident, you understand –'

Eve stared at the other woman. 'If you're going to do it, do it.'

Eve snorted. 'You're in rather a hurry for a lot of pain. It's still early Saturday morning. Nobody will be around for forty-eight hours. Time for you to suffer somewhat.'

She went to the car and leaned in.

Eve pulled at the ropes. Her wrists burned; there was no leeway there. But her ankles weren't so tightly bound.

The other Eve returned, holding a pair of scissors. 'I knew I should have brought a knife for just such occasions, but this will do.'

Eve froze. 'Have you thought about this? Will I commit suicide or am I murdered?'

The other woman snorted. 'You'll be dead either way. And how can I kill myself?' She stepped closer, opening the scissors. 'That reminds me. How did you get here?'

Eve shook her head. 'We're too different. You'll never figure it out.'

She gasped, then bit her lip as pain flared across her belly. The other woman moved back, blood on the scissors.

'I could enjoy this, knowing where to cut, where to slash, where to pierce.' She grinned. 'Tell me how to get to – wherever you come from.'

I am a psychopath. I should have killed my self without warning. I cannot let her – me – know about the books –

Eve cried out. Her left leg kicked, twitched. The pain brought tears to her eyes. The cut was deep in her thigh.

'Next time,' Eve leaned in close to hiss, 'I'll do something to your face. Or your tits. Now tell me.'

Eve shook her head desperately. 'No.'

There was a pop, and she flinched. Another button popped from her blouse.

'That's better.'

She whimpered as the bloodied scissors were wiped across her chest.

'Last chance, sister. Tell me or,' the other Eve laughed, 'I'm sure I needn't spell it out.'

Eve nodded slowly. 'I'll tell you. I'll even take you there.'

The other Eve shook her head. 'Just tell me. If it's true I'll come back for you.' She grinned. 'If it's not, I'll still come back for you.'

Eve shook her head, smiling. 'I don't think so.'

The other Eve was there, scissors against her throat. 'Oh? And why not?'

'For one, I won't tell you where it is. For another, you'll find I changed the exit code on the car park. You won't get out without me.'

--

Eve rebound the fake's wrists behind her back and did her seat belt up. Then she pulled the belt tight and knotted it so the other woman was pressed immobile in her seat.

She slid into the driver's seat, scissors in her left hand. 'This is an automatic. You try anything –' she smiled sweetly at the identical looking woman, 'I'll put the scissors somewhere painful.'

At night the streets of Reading were quiet; the outskirts at least. The closer they got to the centre, the more people were about.

'Where are you taking me? I see a police car, these scissors go in, remember that.'

The other Eve shook her head. 'The edge of town. Market Square. There's a building there.'

A car roared past, swerving at speed, horns blaring, youths in the back staring.

Eve began slowing down, and heard the police siren.

--

Eve pressed back in the seat. The police car was almost upon them, just round the corner behind them. She drew her knees up slowly. Her target had slowed to forty: was still slowing.

As the flashing lights shattered the night, she pushed down even harder and swung her knees to the right, lashing out awkwardly.

There was the sound of burning rubber. Horns. The shriek of metal. And pain exploding everywhere and her own voice screaming and then –

Mask of Morning

He looked so peaceful lying there, arms crossed, cradling the thing to his chest. There was a youthful emptiness to his face, though she guessed he was the wrong side of forty. His hair was shockingly grey, even white in places, with only a few isolated strands of brown.

Halo decided he had probably been quite handsome once. Now his mouth sagged open and a trickle of drool ran down his chin. She wiped it away. He had large hands: she liked that in a man, but there were paler circles of flesh on two fingers of his left hand.

Just my luck. Married and fugued. Disassociated. She tested the straps pinning his torso and legs. Doctor Waterson had wanted his arms strapped down as well, but as she'd pointed out, the patient – her mysterious Mister X – only became violent when they tried to remove it from his arms. She flicked the hair out of her eyes. If only –

'How's he doing, Nurse Brown?'

She turned at the registrar's voice. Dr Samuel – she always thought of him as a *Drrrr* – hated being outvoted by Doctor Waterson. Doctor Waterson cared for patients. Drrrr Samuel stuck his long nose and beady eyes into everything, trying to save money.

'He's not come round yet, Drr-tor.'

Drrrr scowled. 'And you've not succeeded in removing the object from his arms.' His frown deepened. 'If it is what it appears to be, it could make this hospital very famous. The first of its kind, intact –'

'He seems very attached to it, Doctor.'

Drrrr Samuel scowled. 'He's been put out. Have you tried removing it?'

Halo was shocked. 'Doctor. We can't just – it obviously means something –'

Drrrr shook his head. 'If that is authentic, it is far more valuable than any contribution you could make, nurse. More valuable than the poor unfortunate – though I would be interested to know where he got it.'

Halo closed her mouth. It had got her into trouble before, and if she ignored the Drrrr's barbed comments, it was a fulfilling job. When she didn't answer, the Drrrr scowled and stomped off, closing the door quietly.

She reached out a hand to mop the patient's brow – he was staring at her.

'Are you a virgin?'

Halo stared. Blushed. Snorted. They weren't supposed to ask questions like that. She could put her whole life into caring for the unfortunates, but if they started asking questions like that –

He seemed to relax, though his arms still gripped the object tightly. His voice had been rusty, deep. But for the peculiar gleam in his eyes as he'd spoken, his voice could have done something for her.

'My name is Halo. You can call me Nurse Brown. You're in the Prospect Park Hospital in Reading. Do you have a name?'

Mister X shook his head. 'I am a priest of Tonatiuh. I cannot let Tzitzimime win. He will drench the land in my people's blood.'

'Titsme? Who's that?'

He turned to look at her. His eyes were pale brown, but in the antiseptic lighting they looked worn out, rust coloured, faded yellow.

'Tzitzimime. The star demons. They are attacking the sun.' He turned his head and stared out of the window. 'Where are they? Has Tonatiuh been victorious?'

166

Halo shook her head. 'I'll have to get –'

The door opened on cue and Doctor Waterson came in. He always had a sense of timing. In the gentleness of his face he could almost be a patient, but his body was rugged and his mind was sharp.

The left cuff of his shirt was unbuttoned. His tie was askew. Glasses pinched his nose lopsidedly. I'm glad he doesn't wear contacts. Women might notice him. Not that he notices my interest.

'Good morning, Halo. Good morning, sir. How are we today?'

Her patient turned to look at him. 'Are you one of Patecatl's priests?'

Jeremy shook his head unflappably. 'I regret I am not, sir. I am only a humble medic of the mind.'

Jeremy. She rolled her tongue round his name sometimes in the emptiness of her flat at night. Jeremy. Let his name take her where she needed to go.

'Are we victorious?' Her Mister X was asking. 'Has Tonatiuh defeated the Tzitzimime?'

Jeremy – Doctor Waterson – smiled warmly, glancing at her. 'It is daylight outside. Nurse Brown?'

She looked up from her patient. 'Oh. The titsinme. They were attacking the sun. He was worried there would be bloodshed.'

Doctor Waterson smiled at patient X as if it was perfectly normal. Of course, in terms of those in the locked ward, patient X was reasonably sane.

'The sun won. The sacrifices were successful. The sun returned to the land and our people are saved.'

Her patient looked relieved.

'Your people are saved,' Jeremy repeated, gently patting the man's shoulder. 'The sacrifices worked.'

167

The man nodded, stroking the object he held. 'Tonatiuh needed extra strength to fight off the demons. They should both have been virgins but one was enough.'

Halo touched her doctor's arm gently. His shirt sleeve was crisp. For a minute she thought she could feel the blood flowing in his veins.

'Nurse Brown?' he asked quietly.

'The patient asked me if I was a virgin. He seemed – interested.'

Jeremy smiled gently, as if sharing an in-joke. 'Would you say it was lust, or something else?'

Halo blushed. He thinks men lust after me. Most men I've met want me to mother them; protect them from the cruel world.

'I think,' she shook her head. 'I don't think it was lust. Doctor.'

'Thank you, Nurse Brown.' He always kept it polite and formal between them. She'd been in his office once. The walls were filled with diplomas, awards, citations. He was so clever to maintain the appearance that there was nothing between them.

'Can you tell me,' he asked patient X gently, 'about the mask.'

The man stared at him, gripping it tighter to his chest. It glittered dull gold. One edge was stained black and lumpy, somehow distasteful, distorted, out of place.

'I am a priest of Tonatiuh. With this I become Tonatiuh. I needed extra strength to defeat the star demons. They were not of my people, but their sacrifice was worthy. Their sacrifice was successful.' He seemed to relax, though he still gripped the mask tight. 'Their hearts and their blood fed me.'

Halo shivered. His voice was getting stronger. I'm glad he's strapped in. All this talk of sacrifice and virgins.

'Where did all this take place? Where was the place of your victory?'

The patient scowled. 'On top of the pyramid. The works of Tonatiuh are done out of sight of the people. They need the magic and the mystery. I bound the sacrifices to the altars. They came to us at our hour of need. It was midday and the sky was black. Tzitzimime had ambushed me. But they saved my people.'

Jeremy nodded. 'Did they give you their names? Those worthy sacrifices?'

Patient X scowled. 'They were foreign. They had no names.'

There was a knock on the door. Nurse Sheart put her bright, bubbly, blondely offensive head round. 'Doctor Waterson? There's someone here to see you.'

She smiled ingratiatingly at her Jeremy, but directed a scornful sneer at her when the doctor's back was turned.

'I will be back shortly, Tonatiuh. Please excuse me.'

He stepped out of the room with the blonde bitch. In the hallway beyond she saw the tall, white haired, black man who'd brought in patient X. He smiled politely in her direction, baring his teeth. She turned back to the unfortunate.

'Can you tell me about the mask?'

The patient looked at her doubtfully. 'Are you one of my people?'

Halo gritted her teeth and shook her head. 'I'm a foreigner. I'm not a virgin, either.'

Patient X nodded slowly, eyes unfocusing. 'I could not tell my people. They need the mystery. Understanding would destroy them and, in turn, me. But foreigners are incapable of understanding anyway.'

'You can tell me,' she encouraged gently. Jeremy will be so proud of me breaking his shock.

'It is my Godhood.'

169

She stared blankly. 'Your –'

He lifted his face to hers and his eyes were blazing. He was lifting the mask, fitting it over his face.

Halo watched, horrified. I should call –

The mask covered his face perfectly. It was studded with rubies and emeralds. Ornate wings extended to either side; a stylised sun rose above it. It was perfection, only marred by the unsettling black smear that covered the right side.

'I am Tonatiuh.' His voice was harsh, rasping. He twisted and lunged for her. Caught her arm in a painfully tight grip.

'I need to return to my people. I need your strength.'

His other hand ripped, tore, at her tunic. She tried to pull away but his grip tightened: brought tears to her eyes. He swept something off the bedside table with a crash, and there was a spoon in his hands. He lunged at her and Halo froze, terrified.

The door crashed open. Someone was pulling her away. A body was restraining him. His fingers were being levered off her arm. There was a wet sensation and suddenly everything hurt and there were alarm bells and people talking all at once. Halo retreated, hands over her ears.

'It is all right, nurse. What's her name? No. Halo? Halo, can you hear me?'

A hand touched her brow. She was standing by the door. The tall black man was studying her face intently.

'Have a look, Halo. See what you have done.'

Her patient was sitting up, staring at her, crying. The mask fell from his fingers.

'They killed them. They killed them. Butchered them –'

There was something on her. She touched it. Drew her fingers back. They were bloody.

'I'm sorry,' the man wailed. 'I tried to save them. But Karen – oh.' He burst into tears. 'She was so young –'

The black man was talking to her patient calmly, reassuring him.

Nurse Sheart, the harlot, was fussing over Doctor Waterson: he was allowing her to straighten his tie and adjust his glasses. He must be concussed she thought, to allow that little strumpet –

Drrrr Samuel had picked the mask up and was examining it, stroking it. Whatever came over my patient, she thought –

'It is okay, Halo.' The black man stood before her. 'Go to Doctor Waterson's room. I will be there shortly to explain.'

It looked as if Sheart was about to give Waterson mouth to mouth resuscitation. His hand, obviously accidentally, was on her thigh. As she stared, Sheart turned and scowled at her.

The black man practically pushed her out the door. 'Go. Get the wound dressed. Wait for me.'

Waterson's room was as she remembered it, full of smugness and gloating. He would laugh at her in here: he had the blonde strumpet to give him what she should have given him.

The door opened and the tall black man came in.

'You brought – Patient X – in, didn't you?'

He nodded, sitting behind the desk as if it was the most natural thing in the world. 'I wanted to thank you, Halo.' He smiled. 'It is a most unusual and wondrous name. Do you know why your mother gave it to you?'

She shook her head. 'I was brought up in a home. I never knew.'

His smile broadened. She found herself smiling. If he can just take over Waterson's office he must be –

'You have a good affect on the people around you.' His eyes twinkled as he leaned forwards, fingers steepled on the desk. 'You achieved a breakthrough with my client.'

She frowned. 'Your – client.'

If anything his smile broadened, threatening to take the top of his head off. 'I found him. I brought him here. Now I wish to take him to private facilities, and I want to employ you as carer.'

Halo stared. 'What? Leave here?'

He nodded. When he stopped smiling, his face was intimidating. 'It would probably be longer hours, but there would be more pay. You would concentrate just on that one man. And you would have to sign the official secrets act.'

She stared harder. 'Who are you? Is that man a spy?'

The black man shook his head sadly. 'He is just an unfortunate. Caught in the cogs of a wheel we are attempting to halt. He needs caring for. He may give us vital information.'

Halo shivered. 'He kept asking about virginity. And when he put the mask on –'

His grin returned. 'He was in shock. He retreated into the belief he was an Aztec God. Where he got the mask from,' he shrugged. 'But one thing is certain.'

Halo stared at him. 'What?'

He, the mysterious black man, sighed. 'Karen – his daughter – and his wife are dead. Horrifically sacrificed. He either witnessed it or,' he trailed off.

'He was responsible?'

The black man shook his head. 'I would hope not. Not deliberately, anyway. But what he saw pushed him over the edge. A fugue state; disassociation, I believe they call it nowadays.' He shook his head. 'But that is irrelevant. I offered you a job, with no Doctor Samuel or the like. Unlimited budget. What you need, Halo, you would get.'

She stared. 'Why?'

He smiled, taking a business card from his pocket and passing it over. 'There is nothing, no one, for you here. I could use a woman with your abilities.' He grinned. 'I have been studying you for a while, Halo. I may even have answers to questions you have not yet asked. And I think you would fit into the organisation I work for very easily.'

Halo took his card. 'When do I – this is very sudden.'

He nodded. 'When I leave, I take your patient with me. I would like to take my patient's nurse with me as well. Contracts and so forth can be drawn up later, but I offer you as much money and time as you want.'

Sheart the bitch queen had stolen her Jeremy. Jeremy had fallen for it, and he was interested in her patient. So was the Drrrr. She could thwart both of them.

She nodded. 'I will. I'll take it.'

The black man nodded, offering her his hand. 'I knew you would.' He pumped her hand enthusiastically. 'Then let us take your patient. You will report directly to me from now on, Halo, in all things. The name's Randolph. Randolph Wizerbowski.'

Scheherazade and the Caliph's Tale

The courtyard was of a cool, cream-coloured marble. There was not a trace of sand anywhere. At discrete intervals date palms flourished in recessed boxes set into the marble, the moist, black earth and flourishing life contrasting with the pale, lifeless stone. Battlements surrounded the courtyard, ringed with the Caliph's soldiers in silver and black, facing outwards. A fountain dominated the courtyard, of white marble, depicting a tall, handsome bearded man surrounded by seven faithful virgins. The only sound was of tinkling water. The lightest of breezes blew, and the setting sun turned the walls behind her a rosy hue. The gate remained black, blank, featureless. There was no handle on the inside.

Beside the fountain was a large wooden bed. Cushions of swan feathers and throws of peacock feathers were piled up upon it and in its midst sat the Caliph.

The breeze raised goose bumps on her arms. Night was drawing in and the silks they had dressed her in did nothing to keep her warm or give her any modesty.

'So.' The Caliph's voice was thick, like honey or something molten. 'You are my wife.'

She scowled. 'No dowry was mentioned.'

He waved his hand negligently. 'The matter can be discussed tomorrow, for tonight you are my bride.'

Amar shook her head. 'I am here because I had no choice. Are you so desperate for marriage that your men must arrest passing strangers? What of local girls – are there no suitable princesses?'

'I have had princesses,' he boasted, 'they are more spoilt than ordinary girls. They do not make good wives.'

Amar snorted. 'Have you had many brides?'

The Caliph settled his hands on his belly, his eyes cold and small. 'I have not yet found one worthy of my true love. Until I do –'

'If your idea of courtship is having your guards put swords to girls' throats, I'm not surprised you're alone.'

'I'm not alone.' His voice was cold and harsh. 'Tonight, I have you. Tomorrow, I will have another.'

Amar shook her head. 'Bride for a night? I don't think so –'

'I am the Caliph,' he roared, raising himself up onto his knees, looking like nothing so much as a frog. 'You are my chosen bride. It is the greatest honour –'

'I know honour,' she hissed, 'warriors have given their lives, in the dark, alone and unloved, trying to protect their country and their beliefs. There are always threats from the Mongolian Empire and the American Confederacy –'

The Caliph was staring at her, shaking, his eyes narrowing. 'You – you – you'd – dare inter – interrupt me? I am the Caliph. I am –'

'You are an old man. I know boys the match of you.' Amar snorted. 'My son is worth ten of you.'

He looked her up and down, the lust fading from his eyes. 'You are a mother? They told me you were innocent. A virgin.' He wrinkled his nose. 'You are older than I would have chosen –' he reached for a bell set on a small table beside the bed.

Amar took a half step forwards, dropping to one knee. 'I am virgin, my lord. My son is adopted.'

The Caliph froze, his gaze thawing. 'Your son is adopted?'

She bowed her head. 'Yes, Caliph.'

'So you have not borne a child. You have not known a man. You are untouched.'

She kept her gaze on the floor and whispered, 'yes, my lord.'

The Caliph shuffled to the edge of the bed and got up, coming over to examine her. He smelt of oil and figs. His fat fingers caressed her hair, starting at her crown and tracing down to her shoulders, her back.

'I had a wife once,' he whispered, 'she was beautiful. More beautiful than you. Her lips were the colour of warm blood. Her neck was paler than a swan's neck. I had a dress made for her from swans' feathers,' he reminisced. 'It was the finest the tailor ever made. He would have been living in its shadow. I was merciful to him.'

The Caliph sighed wistfully. 'Her eyes were the blue of the ocean when there are depths beneath and the sun above.'

His hands were inside the silken confectionary they'd made her wear. She could still see Mohan's look of terror as the guards led her away.

They will not harm him, she repeated, whilst I do not displease the Caliph. His breath was hot on her neck.

'When she died, I had her shaved. Her hair was braided into a belt.' He abruptly pulled away from her and took a step back.

His belly overhung a wiry, ratty belt that might have been lustrous once, but had long since lost its beauty.

'It was the pinnacle of the belt-maker's craft. To forge a belt from woven strands of silk.' He stepped closer, his hand caressing her hair. 'I may do that for you, Scheherazade. Such hair should not rot in the grave or be burned to the Heavens. Would you like that?'

Amar nodded, stroking the hair belt. 'I would like it, my lord, but we do not need to talk of it yet. I am not unwell; I am relatively young. I will be your wife —'

His hands were on her shoulders, silk thrust aside. 'For one night only,' he finished.

'One night?'

He nodded, stroking her cheek. 'You have beautiful eyes. They may be the most beautiful aspect of you. I will have to preserve them.'

His fingers moved down to her mouth, brushed her lips, slid inside.

Amar held her breath, trying not to choke and fighting the urge to bite as he stroked her teeth, her tongue, the insides of her cheek.

'I examine all the mares I purchase as thoroughly,' he smiled, sickly sweet, and sat on the edge of the bed. 'Come here.'

They know I am the Caliph's bride, even if only for one night. I must escape. Get Mohan to safety.

The rosy light was dying from the sky and stars were twinkling. She locked her jaw against the cold and against the Caliph's investigating fingers.

Amar felt the cold air and couldn't stop the shudder as his fingers probed her intimately.

'Why do you shudder, Scheherazade?'

She forced herself to smile at him, to loosen her tightly clamped jaw. 'I am cold, my lord.'

He shrugged. After a moment he pushed her away. 'You are virgin. But you are older than I would choose. How did you come to adopt a boy?'

Amar remained on her knees. 'He was being misused. He should have been cared for by those who loved him, but they only saw what they could get from him.'

She looked up. The Caliph had gone silent, staring into the distance.

'My lord?' she whispered, laying her hand on his thigh.

He lowered his gaze to look at her. Amar removed her hand.

'I've never had children. I would like a child.'

'I,' she paused cautiously. 'Were there a princess around here, worthy of you –'

The Caliph snorted. Scowled. 'I want no princess bringing up my child. This,' he waved his hands extravagantly and sighed.

Amar shifted until she could sit comfortably, leaning against his leg, her cheek on his knee.

'Are you not comfortable here?'

He stroked her hair absently. 'What lies – beyond the walls? All I see are the guards who protect me, and the secretaries who carry out my wishes, and the viziers who rule in my name.'

She took his hand and kissed his fingers.

'There is a city of good men and women. Humble and extraordinary. Beyond the city is a desert whose sands gleam when the sun shines upon them. Beyond the desert is an ocean teeming with fish and wondrous things. Beyond the ocean,' she sat up on her knees, so that she could look up at him, 'there are other towns, other cities, other worlds, with girls wondrous fair.'

His hands parted her silk. 'I find you fair enough.'

Amar blushed, casting her eyes down. 'My lord, as you say, I am not young. And were I to stand beside you,' she trailed off.

His fingers itched to touch but didn't. 'If you stood beside me?'

'I would have to kneel in your presence, otherwise I would stand as tall. That would be wrong, my lord.'

'Hmm.'

She risked a quick glance up at him. His gaze still lingered on her chest.

'You deserve better than me, my lord.'

179

'Better than you?' His gaze met hers.

Amar gently tugged the silk back across. 'Your soldiers had to arrest me, threaten my son, before I came to you. Your true love would not need such incentive.'

'Your son.'

She nodded slowly. 'You could have my son slain, but my thoughts would remain with him. You need a woman with no attachments who can give all of herself to you.'

'All of herself.' The Caliph tore the silk open and grasped her shoulders. 'I can have the all of you. I will have the all of you.'

He pushed her down. It was a fairly weak push, but Amar lay back, making no move to cover herself.

'You can have any woman you wish, my lord. Why limit yourself to a woman who doesn't love you?'

He snatched up the bell. 'I simply let this ring – no one – No One – has spoken to me like you before.'

'I am not fit for you, my lord. Time you waste here – there is the perfect woman out there for you. She will love you, unreservedly. She will bear your children. She will show you the world beyond this cold garden. I am only her messenger.'

The Caliph stood over her, the bell in his left hand.

'My lord?' she whispered.

He let the bell ring.

An instant later a secretary in black entered, flanked by two black robed Gardeners.

'My lord?' said the secretary, bowing low.

The Caliph gestured at her. 'She came in with another?'

The secretary nodded. 'A guide. A boy child.'

'Bring him here.'

All three withdrew.

The Caliph returned the bell to the table. Night had fallen and the stars glittered coldly. The breeze had dropped but all heat had gone: she was close to shivering.

180

The doors opened again and the secretary and Gardeners returned, bringing with them –

'Mother.'

Mohan burst out of the secretary's grasp and ran to her. She sat up, hugging him one handed, ruffling his hair. He burst into tears and she held him tight as he sobbed into her neck.

'Mama. I was so worried. When they told me you were the Caliph's bride –'

He was gaining height and putting meat on his bones. No longer was he the underfed orphan, unable to grow, unable to age.

Amar smiled. 'It's okay, Mohan. Son.' She looked up at the Caliph. 'What will you do with us?'

The Caliph looked at the secretary. 'I want to explore this city of mine.'

The secretary frowned. 'It's not safe, my lord. It is night and there are many undesirables –'

'My lord,' said Amaranthaceae, 'you are the Caliph. You can do what you please. If you wish, I will act as your bodyguard.'

The secretary snorted. 'You're a woman.'

She looked up at the Caliph. 'I was a Janissary officer before I became a woman.'

The Caliph looked at the secretary. 'He would keep me in here. Prove your words, woman.'

'My lord, you cannot –'

'It will be fine, Mohan. Don't worry.' She kissed her son's forehead.

The secretary backed away but was held by the Gardeners.

She stepped closer and he tripped up. She rode him down. As he opened his mouth to scream, she twisted his head sharply.

Amar stood up and held out her hand for Mohan. 'I will be your bodyguard, my lord, but I should dress appropriately. When I am ready, will you accompany me into your city?'

The Caliph gazed at the body of his previous secretary. 'Take that away,' he ordered. He turned his gaze to her. 'You could have raised a hand at any time. To kill like that –'

Amar held out her hand to Mohan again. 'I do what I must to protect my son.'

The Caliph frowned. 'Still I would not have your loyalty.' He sighed. 'You have one week. Your son will remain with me. If, after that time, you have not found my perfect life mate –' his eyes glittered greedily, drinking in her as-good-as nudity – 'I will make you my wife, and then the following morning you will watch your son die. And then you will die.' He pulled Mohan over to sit beside him. 'You may go.'

Amaranthaceae blew her son a kiss. 'I will be back in under a week, Mohan. Keep the Caliph entertained while I find him the perfect bride.' She inclined her head to the Caliph. 'I will find your perfect wife and return with her, within a week. This I swear,' she said, meeting the Caliph's gaze, 'as a Janissary and a mother.'

Xenology Codex

'Mrs Rhoad?'

She looks up at her name. She has blue eyes, a skeletal frame. Scarecrow black hair fading to white, the ends blonde. She half smiles, sensing a customer, then sees the book under your arm. She blushes, staring.

'I'm afraid that book is not –'

You cut her off with a wave of your hand. 'I have a receipt,' you tell her, aware of the customers in the bookshop, 'it was sold to me by a member of your staff. I would like to discuss it with you.'

She looks flustered. You would guess her age at late forties. Strong and independent you think, but failing in looks and life. Husband left her for a younger woman – or a man – and now even the shop is getting too much for her.

'I wondered where it had gone. I'll gladly refund your money; it shouldn't have been sold –'

'But it was,' you continue, aware others are listening: the shop has the air of a library, 'and I had it investigated.'

You wait as she apologises to the customers, easing them out of the shop. You put the heavy, old, book down on the counter.

The shop has a slightly abandoned look to it, like it has seen better days. You see dust on the shelves, mustiness in the air and chewing gum on the floor. But it's got that smell, like the libraries of old when information was only available in hardcopy.

But as for Jacaranda –

She wears earrings. You'd bet ten to a penny she's got tattoos beneath the jeans and blouse she wears. She's not quite as you imagined; as you suspected she would be. There's certainly no sense of otherworldliness. Which is good. Or very, very bad.

But then you know nothing of that, either. You're here because you're a fixer. An arranger. And you've found a source of authentic aged paper. You imagine there's people you know – dangerous people – who would pay good money for that. That's your way in to her. You can make her rich. Gain her confidence.

It's a perfect cover, you think. The height of respectability: a bookshop. Where the learned classes come. You're surprised no one has thought of it before.

Perhaps it's a bad day for her. You had her and her past thoroughly checked out. Her family you found almost as interesting as what you bought here last time.

Mrs Rhoad returns, a tired expression on her face.

'It was all a joke,' she begins, but you hold up your hand to stop her.

'You do not have to lie to me, Mrs Rhoad. May I call you Jacaranda? Such an unusual name. But then,' you smile meaningfully, 'such an unusual family.'

She frowns but doesn't speak. She might look like a down-at-heels sales assistant, but you know better. She's clever, and very skilled, or got contacts who are anyway.

'I am Wadsworth. Excelsior Wadsworth.' You smile. 'No relation to but named after the poet. And you? Why did your mother choose Jacaranda as your name?'

She stares at you, nonplussed. 'I don't really –' she shakes her head. 'What do you want?'

You see the flash of intelligence in her eyes. 'Good. You say this is a fake,' and you pat the locked book, 'but I have had it checked. The paper is well over two hundred years old.'

She looks at you, thin lipped. She might have been a beauty in her youth, but you find her nose too thin, her cheeks too shallow. There's no meat to her, but then she's not lunch.

'I would be interested – financially interested – in purchasing a stock of such paper. Or the skills of whoever created it.'

She shakes her head. She disappoints you by lying. 'The book is a fake, a joke present. I don't know why you think –'

'Henghist Goring and Horsa Streatley,' you interrupt. 'Only now it is Henghist Road. Strange that your husband should change his name to yours and misspell it simultaneously.'

At six foot you don't tower over her: she's about five nine. But you've a bulk she doesn't.

'Stranger still –' you smile, the way a shark smiles when it sees its prey, 'strangeness seems to surround you. Do you know who Henghist and Horsa really are?'

She stares, eyes narrowed. You've hit target but she's too clever to speak, too slow to stop the automatic reaction.

'You have a very interesting family, Jacaranda. A husband who doesn't exist; no birth certificate. A brother in law the same, now deceased.'

'I really don't,' she begins, but you wave her into silence. 'None of this really matters. I simply wish – and I am willing to purchase off you – a stock of similarly aged paper, or the skills required to create it.'

She shakes her head. 'The paper isn't that old. Thirty years, maybe. I don't know why your tests –'

'Interesting,' you interrupt, 'that a joke present – presumably from your husband – should have his pre-matrimonial name and your brother in law's on it.' You grin. 'And joke though you claim it to be, the contents are interesting.'

She says nothing. She is stronger than she appears, but she's female. She can easily be broken, if you can find her weak spot.

'Perhaps you do not understand me, Mrs Rhoad. I thought I was making myself clear. I wish to purchase paper of a similar age, or the skills to create it. I will pay handsomely.'

She shakes her head, exasperated. 'It isn't that old. The book's not even mine –' she breaks off.

'I take it it belongs to your husband, now your brother in law is dead.'

She nods reluctantly.

'Good. You say the paper is thirty years old. Scientific testing proves it is well over two hundred. Is your husband a forger?'

She stares: snorts in a believable fashion. 'Henghist? No. He's a liar and a twister, but –' she breaks off again.

You are beginning to get annoyed with her. You want to slap her, at least, but it's too public. You imagine the character you're playing would pay almost any price for authentic forged paper like that. With it you can make an even greater killing.

'Think very carefully, Mrs Rhoad. If you know where I can get a supply of paper like this –' you don't smile: she stands between you and hundreds of thousands of pounds of easy profit. 'Just give me a name, an address, of the person who created it, and I will make you a wealthy woman.'

She shakes her head disappointingly. She still claims it is not that old.

You hold up your hand to stop her. 'Enough. If you will not trade or share your sources with me,' you'd hoped it wouldn't come to this, 'then a young woman in Bristol will be receiving a visit from some,' you pause, smile, in your most charming way, 'ah, associates of mine.'

She stares at you blankly. 'I have no idea what you're talking about. I think it would be best if you leave now.'

Can it be that she doesn't know about Bridget? No. She is too clever for that. Double bluff, you decide, or simple tiredness.

'Must I spell it out for you?' She isn't as clever as you thought if you're being condescending to her. 'Your niece, Bridget, although I believe she prefers the name Bridge.'

Her jaw drops. She stares. She didn't know. You curse mentally. 'One call, and she will be –'

'No.' Jacaranda pushes herself away from the counter, sweeping the codex out of your reach. 'The book is mine and you will not harm my niece or anyone I know. Go, Excelsior, go now and do not return. It will not be safe for you.'

Her eyes are flashing, not blue but diamond sapphire. Her tiredness, her ignorance, her confusion, is gone.

'This is my bookshop. Do not think that you can walk into my domain and throw your weight around. Others have tried,' and her eyes narrow, and she's not speaking empty words, you can tell, 'and others have failed. Others no longer walk this earth.'

She takes a step towards you and you back away.

'This is not just a bookshop, Excelsior.'

Her voice is low, dark, malevolent. Threat and promise wrapped in pure velvet. You expected her to have backup, protection, not to be capable herself.

'This is where the wild things converge. You think you can bully and threaten; that this is just a bookshop and I am just a shop owner.'

She laughs and you feel cold. Is it your imagination or is the shop floor darker?

'This is not just a bookshop and I am not just a shop owner and you are in deeper than you imagine.'

She takes a step towards you and you turn.

'Run, little man.'

You break for the door. Her laughter breaks forth behind you, carrying you out of the door and away, away from –

When you catch your breath, when you stop running, you are several streets away. You underestimated her, badly. But even so – you smile. You've actually met her. Met Her. The one who will –

You didn't tell her it all. That is good. She might know – she must know – but you're not sure. Maybe she doesn't know.

You'll have to be more careful, and a lot cleverer, if there is to be a next time. She knew Henghist and Horsa weren't real, knew they didn't officially exist.

'But she didn't know – or didn't reveal that she didn't know – that official records have no trace of her either. No birth certificate. No school records. Nothing until she was fifteen, when she sprang, fully formed, into Reading.'

You shake. Giving her Bridget – Bridge – was such a little thing. And if it draws her out of the bookshop, it will be worth it. Because if she and the bookshop aren't stopped, then all realities will suffer.

Deo in Ascendance

The sun was warm on her back. She straightened up, sweeping the hair back from her face. Angeli insisted on braiding her hair into long plaits, but she preferred it loose, a living waterfall of black silk.

Lakshmi smiled. Angeli had married a good man in Bishal. Their three sons thrived, fit and healthy. He didn't ask why Angeli shared the nursing with her, when she was fully capable. It freed her up, and Lakshmi worked in their fields for nothing. He never once asked, trusting his wife, not wanting to offend her.

Life in the village – was better than it had been. Fewer children died and all the villagers knew but no one spoke out loud that it was because Lakshmi nursed their young. They had their fields, and their few animals, and some of the men occasionally got work portering and everything else was a blessing from the Goddess. They didn't question, just worked all the more diligently.

Lakshmi turned back to the field. For the first time last year the village had been able to send a child to school. The whole village had gathered to watch them walk down the hillside – and gathered again in the evening to watch them return.

Angeli had spoken to her that night, of the hope that she and Bishal would have a daughter and that her daughter would go to school.

Lakshmi had embraced her and for a moment or two Angeli had clung to her in wordless love, trust, hope, gratitude and fear for the future. She had gone out into the night then, to give her adopted daughter and husband some privacy, although it would not have occurred to them to ask. Sex was private but Lakshmi was Angeli's mother and everyone knew Lakshmi wasn't –

Lakshmi sighed. She wasn't Nepalese. She wasn't Western or Chinese or Mongol and yet she had become part of their village.

Her children, her birth children, Ahimsa and Karma, were fully integrated Nepalese, with families of their own. But the young couples of the village were her children now.

Angeli was seventeen, and proud mother of three healthy, strong boys. Yet she hadn't been expected to survive beyond a few months old. With her survival the young mothers of the time had come to her and Lakshmi had found herself a home, a place, a meaning.

She finished planting and put the woven bowl down. Her fingers were sweaty. A warm wind blew down the mountainside and she turned. She had lived up there, remote, separate, for too long. Now she was part –

Lakshmi lifted and tilted her head. There was always the sound of wind in the trees but that had fallen away. The mountain was silent. Still. Unnatural.

She turned and ran for the centre of the village. The wall of mani stones wouldn't protect the village. They were for belief. But what was coming –

The air was suddenly alive with a roaring sound. Far, far above an avalanche had begun.

She watched as the trees were shredded. A living carpet of rocks demolished them, moving on down. If it hits the village – Lakshmi looked around. No wall, no house, would withstand them.

Other villagers had returned, were gathering about her. A few were running away, hoping to avoid the onslaught. A hand slipped into hers: the village elder, a worried look on his face. Other hands touched her, gripped her arms, lay against her back, as if she were an anchor in the storm.

The avalanche came on slowly, the air heavy with the sounds of death and destruction, of ultimate conclusion.

The air was suddenly shrieking with tiny stones, shrapnel flung far ahead of the approaching tidal wave. Someone offered her a cloak: she pushed it back, barely noticing the cuts as the wind-lashed stones tore at her face, her chest, her arms. Villagers huddled behind her, but in the sounds of destruction Lakshmi heard –

She gently disentangled the hands and stepped away from her only family. They made to follow but she shook her head, walking away from them.

A larger stone sliced her cheek open. Angeli screamed, made to run to her. Others understood and held her fast.

Lakshmi backed away. I will not turn my back on them.

The direction of the avalanche was changing, moving off to one side.

The thunder of stones parted the skin of her fingers. Shredded the heavy skirt. Slashed at her thighs and lacerated her chest.

She strode faster. Less than half the village would be caught by the avalanche. The village elder was moving his people back, three restraining Angeli, who was screaming hysterically.

The ground was shaking. The avalanche was almost upon the village but it had turned to one side. A few houses would be destroyed but no one would die.

The tidal wave swept her off her feet. There was pain, but only pain of the body. The body had simply been a vessel for a soul; a soul whose time had not come.

Her eyes were filled with dust and her mouth with rock shrapnel and she could feel the streams of blood, like prayer flags flapping out behind her, as the avalanche tore into her body.

'I said I would find you.'

His voice filled her and she threw back her head, crying joyously. The pleasure was far beyond the physical as his voice made her soul sing.

'I have never been far from you and now the time is right.'

A boulder took her off her knees.

'The time is right to come back, to remember.'

She was rising above herself. Her body – was an empty cage.

'Remember it is all a matter of time. Of timing.'

The avalanche shredded what was left of her body, but what had been Lakshmi had long gone.

Mirror of Illusion

'I'd give you my hand, but I'm not sure you'd take it.'

Bridge looked up. A group of winos sat with their backs to the half collapsed wall, a fire in a metal bucket burning weakly in front of them. Three of them wore layers of rags and carrier bags and gazed mutely at the fire. One stretched his hands out, only to be growled at by one of the others. The fourth –

Bridge stared. The bottle was still in her pocket, weighing heavily against her hip, its cap unopened. It offered blissful release, freedom, security, an escape from the pain –. She blinked.

He – it – was still there. She pulled her jacket sleeve up. Pinched her arm until tears burst from her eyes.

'Why? Why?'

He was sitting beside the winos as if he was one of them. As if it was perfectly natural. As if he was real.

Wings trailed in the filth and the dirt. The hem of his garment was stained with mud and ash. There was dirt on his hands. He sat, legs crossed, hands in his lap, not looking up at her. Golden, curly hair that had smoke and fire debris in it.

Bridge shook her head. She had a sudden desire to throw the bottle at him, to disprove him. But it would be a waste. It was solace. She needed the bottle. Without it, the pain –

'Take my hand, Bridge. Take it.'

She staggered backwards. He was looking up at her, eyes all molten water and fiery ice. She shook her head desperately, clutching at the bottle.

'No. No,' she sobbed. 'You're just –'

Bridge turned and ran.

--

Her mouth burned. That was the mistake in not keeping alcohol in the house. Sobering up. If she kept drinking it'd never hurt. The bridge would be beyond her abilities –

She screwed her eyes up. Samantha. Somewhere, out there, beyond the bridge, her daughter waited, deprived, denied, destroyed too soon.

Samantha. I never wanted to – I always looked. I thought, in time, you would come to me. Or you'd moved on. A happier place. She groaned, pressing her face into the pillow, stretching her arms out.

Something cold and hard touched her hand. She traced its contours, fingers suddenly wet, the smell making her head pound as she grasped the neck of the bottle.

Bridge opened her eyes; turned her head. The bottle was half drunk, spilled out on the bed. She pulled it to her; raised it to her lips. The whiskey burned away her headache, her pain. She could feel its warmth spreading through her, tingling, its warmth destroying the coldness that had for so long seemed natural; seemed normal.

There was something in her hand. The bed sheet. She pulled her hand away, aware it felt wrong, not like the sheet at all.

Bridge lowered the bottle. Everything was fuzzy but everything was warm. Warm was good.

There were – feathers – in her hand. She groaned, turning to look at the pillow. 'I must have –'

The pillows were intact.

She lifted her hand. The feathers streamed from it, twisting and turning, caught in a breeze she couldn't feel. They were golden. White. Albino. Slowly fading to grey.

Bridge stared at what was left. Dust. Dust that shone even as it disintegrated.

The warmth left her dry mouthed and coughing. She kicked the almost empty bottle away, trying not to breathe in the stink of alcohol.

She pulled herself out of bed and staggered for the door. 'The angel. Did I really see an angel?'

The shower intensified her headache but washed away some of the smell; washed away the dirt from her fingers.

'Why am I seeing angels? What does it mean?'

--

The winos were still there. Bridge let out her breath, unaware she'd been holding it. There were five in total, squatting round the bucket of fire.

'Excuse me. Were any of you here last night?'

They muttered to themselves, ignoring her. The stink of filth about them was almost as strong as the smell of alcohol.

'I'll,' she hesitated, 'I'll buy a meal for whoever talks to me about last night.'

One of them growled, looking up and over her shoulder. 'What'n use food? Not for'n all the food in Frenchie land.'

A couple passed by, looking at her oddly.

She waited until they were out of earshot. 'There was someone with you last night. There was three of you – and him.'

Another looked up at her. 'Juice three of uus last night. Juice three.'

'No. There was a fourth. A voice like.' She closed her eyes. 'A voice like a bell. Or a trumpet.' She shook her head. 'He was wearing a robe. He had wings. You must –'

'I wish the council would do something about the winos. They're spoiling the city centre. This used to be an upmarket area.'

Another couple passed, sneering at her openly.

One of the winos had got to his feet and reached into his shabby coat, removed a bottle. 'Some of this, and yule be seeing things again. Whatever you want to see.' He belched; tottered away unsteadily.

Bridge sighed. 'I'll buy a bottle for anyone who can tell me about the angel.'

One of the winos chuckled. 'I'll tell yer. I saw's an angel once. She had big tits.'

A couple of the others sniggered. Bridge turned away.

'Come on, miss. If you haven't got a refuge to go to –'

Two policemen closed in on her.

--

She was standing on the bridge. It was collapsing around her in a rain of feathers.

Bridge sat up. She was in her own bed, bathed in sweat. The Police had let her off with a warning. She'd come home. Tidied up and cleaned, aired the bedroom until it no longer smelt of whiskey.

She'd been thinking about Samantha. Been looking at photos of her. Crashed out.

And woken up, dreaming of the end of the bridge and angels.

Bridge rubbed her cheeks. 'Am I losing it?' She massaged her forehead. 'Was I drinking – before the night before last? Did I imagine seeing the angel?'

I went to the shop. I bought a bottle of whiskey. The teller remembered me. We talked a while. I headed home; saw the angel. Did I drink in the shop? Was I already drunk then?

She went through to the bathroom, shedding clothes as she went. Got into the shower and turned it on. There was a groaning, thumping, sound from the boiler. Bridge turned to face it, frowning, and the showerhead exploded into life behind her.

She turned back, gasping, as feathers washed over her, tangling in her hair, filling her mouth and cascading over her. They were prickly and arousing at the same time and as she swept them from her skin they crumbled to dust. Water, near boiling, burst from the showerhead, and she gasped. The heat flushed her skin and she turned her head, sluicing the sweat and feathers away.

She dressed and went down to her office. The curtains were already closed so she sat down, closed her eyes and concentrated.

It was different. Difficult. Normally she had someone with her, and their spirit used hers as a conduit. On her own –

Bridge blinked. The room had gone cold. Her hands on the table, palms down, were trembling.

She closed her eyes. Samantha. Samantha, where are you? I am Bridget. Your mother. The gatekeeper. Samantha?

She couldn't find the bridge. Couldn't get to it. Something stopped her, blocked her access. She shook her head. I have to get to the bridge. If I can find Samantha –

'She is beyond you.'

Her eyes flew open. A wino sat opposite her. Only his voice –

His hair was ragged, receding. His wings were gone. There was a hint of robe, but it was grubby grey, overlaid with mismatched layers of tattered clothing.

'You.' She stared. 'You're the angel.'

He – it – whatever – half shrugged. 'I am what you make me. You abandoned me.'

Bridge shook her head desperately. 'No. I thought I imagined it. I thought I was drunk. No one remembered you.'

He placed his hands on the table. His fingernails were ripped and torn, the fingers grubby. 'No one sees me but you.'

She stared. 'Am I mad? The bridge – I was trying to get to the bridge.'

He frowned. 'Alcohol impedes you. You impede yourself. You prevent yourself deliberately.'

197

Bridge scowled. 'No. I want to see my daughter. I want to know why –'

'They are looking for you.'

She stared. Froze. Tried to control the trembling. 'Who?' she whispered.

The angel smiled. 'A time of conflict is coming. A conjunction of many forces. It concerns you. You should be there.'

Bridge stared. 'Who are you? How do you know this? Who looks for me?'

He laughed, and for an instant she could see the power, the majesty, in his gaze again. 'You know who I am. The bridge will be denied you until this is resolved. The Unforsaken Land is not for you. You are remembered. You are being searched for.'

'Who?' she demanded, rising to her feet.

I cannot protect myself against my mentor. His former employees want me. He is a potential every time I go to the bridge, but I go anyway. I will not bring him back. Not when I cannot even see my own daughter.

'Your father.'

Bridge stared. 'No. He left. He died. Mother –' she cringed, remembering the whippings and the punishments inflicted whenever she'd mentioned her strange dreams or premonitions of the bridge between life and death.

'Your father searches for you,' the angel continued, leaning forwards, his voice suddenly warmer, 'as does your aunt. You would be wise to find her.'

Bridge stared. 'My father is alive?' She gripped the edge of the desk tight.

The angel nodded.

Bridge wondered when he'd become bald. His fingers were twisted; more like claws.

'Your father is alive and searches for you now more desperately than ever before. Your aunt never stopped looking for you.'

Bridge frowned. 'I was – after university – I ran away –'

'– and he found you,' the angel continued, 'your mentor. He erased all trace of Bridget. Created Bridge in her absence, laying one false trail over the one he erased. It was a few years before Horsa realised you were missing.'

Bridge shook her head. 'My father. He's been looking for me?'

'As has Jacaranda. Both have –' he paused – 'unique forces at their disposal. Without you, things will be unbalanced.'

Bridge went to sit down, then realised she was already. 'Auntie Jac is looking for me also?' She had always liked the bookish Jacaranda for her slight unworldliness.

The angel nodded. He had an unshaven chin; his fingers were scourged with arthritis. 'A conjunction is coming. Apocalypse. Armageddon. Call it what you will. Different realities are bleeding through. Soon, the dam will burst.' He smiled suddenly. 'Or should I say the bookshop.'

Bridge blinked. 'What should I do?'

'You would ask me?'

She nodded. 'Yes. Since you're me. My conscience, or soul, or something.'

There was a soft noise, of muffled feathers, and then the room was empty but for her and a mass of scattered feathers, slowly descending. She reached out and caught one. Pure white.

Jacaranda. Horsa.

Both were looking for her.

There was only one place they would be.

Reading.

Empire in the name of

To the north, the land dropped down to the Tames. The market town of Redinge sprawled ungainly on its banks. Beyond the Tames the land rose once more to the Downs. To the north and west lay Walingeford; to the north and east Oxeneford.

He would rather have headed to Oxeneford: the chance to visit his sister Alicia was rare. But Rufus commanded and you showed enthusiasm. Wintour shuddered. You showed enthusiasm or Rufus had done to you what he'd had done to other knights or barons who he believed had failed him.

To the south the ground was marshy. A few slovenly Saxon hovels were scattered here and there. He wrinkled his sunburned nose. The natives were as foul smelling as their ale.

To the east the ground levelled out, leading in straight roads and rambling byways to Windesores and the King's castle.

Wintour shuddered again. Some other of Rufus' knights were little better than the Saxons they were trying to civilise. Boorish, rutting idiots, their brains in their breeches.

To the west, beyond the small tower-like castle, the countryside opened up, leading to rolling hills. A mile hence farmland gave way to forest – thick, ungainly, sprawling: Louse Hille, where the rebels were gathering their forces.

Alfred rode out to meet him. The constable of Redinge had only a small force, no more than a hundred men from knights to servientes: the servientes would be as nothing to the rebels.

He had pale red hair. Saxon ancestry no doubt. But he'd held the position well for a number of years. Weather beaten face with a scar down one cheek. The air of a warrior: aging, but not yet past it.

He watched as Alfred looked past him to the force he commanded, his eyes widening as he took in the banners and escutcheon. The constable looked surprised. His troops were openly staring.

'Wintour of Banesberie greets Alfred, constable of Redinge. I come in the King's name.'

Alfred inclined his head. His castle was little more than a tower of stone with earthen walls overlooking the town and the Tames crossing.

'You honour me, Sir Wintour. But your company seems a little – oversized – for the problem.'

Wintour frowned. 'Oh? While the death of Archbishop Ranulf and Guy de Guiswardine was no loss to the king, the fact that the rebels are heading for Windesores and gathering recruits all the time is cause for concern.' He twitched. 'I am commanded to stop them here and then continue on to Shrewsbury to assist Belleme.'

Alfred seemed confused. 'I sent word to His Majesty. The town of Redinge,' he shuddered. 'I am not given to nightmares or phantasms, and I am not the only one who has experienced them.'

Wintour looked past him. Louse Hille was only a mile away or so, the land mostly open between them. It would be difficult for the rebels to approach unseen: difficult, also, for scouts to track them unobtrusively.

'Tell me, Alfred. Is there a path to either side of Louse Hille?'

The constable seemed to gather his wits. 'There is not. It is a dark place, full of malevolent spirits and steep hillsides. The land rises behind. While it commands a good view, anyone within cannot approach the town openly.'

He frowned. 'What is this talk of malevolence, spirits and phantasms?'

Alfred shuddered. 'I have commanded Redinge for a number of years, by the King's grace. It is a small market town,

most valuable for the river crossing. But in the last year or two –
' he crossed himself.

Wintour shrugged. 'Such tales can wait. My men need
food and watering. We cannot charge the rebels: we must draw
them out.'

Alfred nodded slowly. 'There may be a way. The river
Kenet – little more than a stream in places – runs in that
direction, though to the west of the woods. The land undulates.
A small force could use it, though,' he paused. 'May I speak
bluntly, my lord?'

Wintour nodded, motioning to his captains to let his
men stand easy.

'No rebels – no body – would choose to linger in Louse
Hille longer than necessary. It is difficult to find verderers to
patrol it. It is said to be the dwelling place of an ancient Anglo
Saxon God – Cernunnos.'

Wintour dismissed the notion with a grunt, beckoning
one of his knights forward. 'Assemble a scouting party, Warrene.
Send them along the Kenet. I want to know if the rebels are in
the forest.'

Warrene bowed and withdrew.

'Now, Alfred. I want quarters, food, a fire, a wench. My
men can pitch camp here, but my knights will require quarters,
stabling, a smithy – the usual.'

The constable nodded. 'Of course, my lord. I will arrange
it.'

--

Later, with a roaring fire in the guest room and a wench sleeping
insensate in his bed, Wintour summoned Alfred. His squire had
removed his armour and his boots. Now he stretched stockinged
feet towards the fire.

There was a knock at the door. At his call, Alfred entered.

'Your knights are settled in quarters, Sir Wintour. My men are furnishing yours with food. The Tames Valley is fertile: they will dine well, if plainly. It is not as rich an area as Windesores or Shrewsbury.'

Wintour nodded absently. 'You know nothing of these rebels?'

Alfred looked half shocked, as if he was implying he supported them. The older man shook his head. 'No, my lord. Traders – merchants – are unsettled. I have been trying to resolve that conflict. There is something in Redinge,' he shrugged, 'it prickles the nerves. Puts men at one another's throats.'

'Your – phantoms?' he paused.

The constable nodded but he continued.

'That is not why the king has sent me. The Marcher castle at Guiswardine was gutted. The lord was a lowly one; his death presents Rufus with an opportunity and a reason. That was where I was headed, until we heard that the rebels – a mix of outlaws and the lord's turncoat men – were headed towards Windesores. First, they will be defeated, and then for the nerve of the Welsh in attacking a Norman lord,' he paused. Shook his head. 'It is better you do not know the full plans of the King.'

Alfred shook his head. 'I knew none of this, my lord. As I said, the town of Redinge –'

Wintour dismissed his comments. 'You are constable of Redinge and that is rightly your main concern. But this is bigger than that. Treason and unrest. Rufus does not take kindly to such things.'

Alfred nodded. 'I gave what assistance I could to your scouts; they will be some time in returning. May I at least show you Redinge? It is not much to a lord accustomed to cathedral towns and the king's court, –'

He sighed. If it will stop him prattling. 'Yes, Alfred. Be warned though. Behind most stories of spirits and spectral haunting are acts of malfeasance. I expect no less from this.'

The constable shrugged. 'I will have horses readied, my lord. When you are ready.'

--

It barely deserved to be called a town. There was a crude market, mostly selling farm produce and animals. A few houses in scattered blocks, mostly wooden Saxon dwellings; only a few stone-built. A small church, rustic and surprisingly charming, overlooking a tributary of the Tames.

'Do you know what the source of this – unease – is?'

Wintour could see something in the faces of the peasants. They recognised Alfred: moved aside for them. Some even called him by name: a few he replied to. This was a master butcher. He was the best fisherman for pike. She was an embroiderer of note.

But in their faces was an ingrained wariness, an unease. Not of him. Not seeds of rebellion. He'd seen enough of that doing Rufus' business over the years. The peasants' unease was of a different breed.

'It.' Alfred seemed curiously reluctant to speak. 'It is strongest in the old marketplace. That is why there is a separate fish market and a cattle market. They prosper but the market place –' he indicated with a flourish the wide earthen area between two shambolic lines of dwellings. The one at the end was a rich merchant's dwelling. Another was a public house. Beside it a wheelwright. Nothing untoward. Nothing unexpected.

It was late evening. The sun was sinking into the west, casting long, bloody, shadows before it. The chamber at the castle had been warm, the woman a pleasing use of different muscles after the hard ride from Windesores.

Wintour didn't like evenings. He never had. All that waiting for the morning and combat. It would be different if he had a noble lady; a domain to call his own. But he was Rufus' man, and settled family life wasn't part of Rufus' plan for him.

Redinge might be bucolic, but it was far better than Shrewsbury would be. De Belleme was an even worse master than Rufus, though he didn't pity the Welsh. They have brought their own pain and destruction down upon themselves by attacking Guiswardine.

A screaming owl startled him out of his thoughts and he looked up. They'd barely seemed to move – were still in the marketplace – but it seemed darker. Rats ran in the shadows. Bats shot past like bolts from crossbows.

Most of the traders had gone but a few remained, standing round a blazing fire. He could smell the rubbish being burnt, and stale food, and the stink of sweaty bodies.

Alfred led the way towards the fire, the clinking of the horses' harnesses loud in the night. The men parted before them.

'A good day's takings?' enquired the constable.

One man grunted. Another shrugged. A third made the sign of horns.

'There were strangers in the market place earlier. Heathens. Devils.'

'Strangers?' Wintour enquired.

The merchant looked past Alfred to him. 'Three women. Skin as black as night. Ugly as sin.'

'Why did you call them heathens?' asked the constable.

The man scowled. 'They weren't no Christian folk. The way they walked.' His voice trembled. 'And they carried arms,' he added in a hushed voice.

'Female warriors?' Wintour snorted. 'A likely tale. What were you supping?'

The man glared at him. 'I ain't no toper. The things I've seen these past months.' He shook his head. 'Hell is coming to Redinge.'

Others were nodding. Peasant foolishness, superstition.

'Does anyone know where they came from? Where they were going? Did any of you actually speak to these – women?'

The thought of Alicia or any woman bearing arms was laughable. I'll mention it in my report. The constable should have crushed such nonsense, not be taken in by it.

'I spoke to one of them.'

Wintour looked at the speaker. By his discoloured clothes and stained hands he guessed the man a dyer. 'Go on.'

'I spoke to one, about a month ago. He spoke heathen lingo. Didn't make sense. Only one word I understood. Armageddon.'

He shrugged. 'Do you know Latin? Or French? The man sounds religious. He was probably quoting scripture. Could have been a pilgrim.'

The dyer shook his head but didn't answer.

He turned, hand on sword hilt, even before he became aware that he was hearing hoof beats. Two men galloped into the marketplace – one his man, the other of the constable.

'My lord,' his man snapped, 'you'd best return to the castle. There's been an attack.'

--

The damage wasn't as bad as he'd feared. Some of the horses had bolted: his servientes were out chasing them. A couple of dozen foot soldiers were dead, including one squire. Fires had been scattered, but the grass was too close cropped to catch. His men were milling around, bullish, ebullient.

'Warrene,' he bellowed.

The knight came running, in half chain, anger on his face.

'What happened?'

Warrene scowled. 'They came down the main track. They knew,' his gaze shifted to the constable for an instant, 'we were told they were farmers. They had a cart. As they approached,' he snapped his fingers.

A servientes came running, carrying something almost invisible. Warrene handed it to him. It was a three foot long arrow, the tip blooded, the fletching ripped.

'What's so special about an arrow?' asked the constable.

Wintour glanced at the man. 'It's a longbow arrow. Welsh. Damn.' If the Welsh have joined, if this is anything more than one renegade band – but how could they have got this far? From Marcher lands to Southern England, they've crossed a fair tract through the midlands.

'That's not all,' said Warrene.

'What?'

The knight looked uncomfortable. 'During the fighting – we – I don't know how –'

'Get on with it.'

Warrene swallowed. 'We found the heads of the scouts in the courtyard. I've organised a full search of the castle, but there's no sign of how they got inside.'

'Alfred. I want words with you. Inside.'

The constable nodded, dismounting.

'How many of theirs did we get?'

Warrene shook his head. 'Their archers kept ours at bay. I sent such cavalry as was ready, but they shot the horses out from under them.'

'Secure the castle. Secure the grounds. Place a guard on the Kenet, just in case. I want rings of lit torches for a quarter mile in all directions.'

He stomped off, following Alfred into the castle. Warriors scurried across the courtyard.

'Your chamber will do.'

The constable's chamber wasn't much larger than his. He didn't want to warn the man by drawing his sword. As the man turned, he placed the point of his dagger against his neck. The constable stared.

'They came from the Kenet. My scouts must have gone straight into them. Those on patrol here were told they were farmers.' He shook his head. 'You have been trying to blindside me, with nonsense tales of apparitions and uneasy feelings. You wanted me absent. Hoped without me those you're allied to could make the first move. Well, it didn't work.'

'My lord, I must protest my innocence. I knew nothing of this –'

He nodded slowly, removing the dagger.

The constable breathed a sigh of relief. 'Thank you, my lord. I –'

Wintour drove the knife into the man's guts, twisting it upwards. The constable stared, gagging. A bubble of blood burst upon his lips. He gave the dagger one final push, then stepped back, letting the body fall to the floor.

Wintour opened the door and called for Warrene. The knight was with him in moments.

'Alfred, at least, was in league with the rebels. I do not know or trust his men. We cannot stay here. His men must stay here, under guard, while we tackle the rebels head on.'

'They have Welsh bowmen, my lord.'

He looked at the knight. 'Our greatest mistake would be entering Louse Hille. Hills and trees. Natural terrain for the Welsh. But there is a broad plateau below the wood's edge. They will overshadow us, but we will be beyond the reach of their archers.'

Warrene nodded slowly. 'In the gallop uphill –'

Wintour shook his head. 'We will let them descend upon us. We will force them to descend upon us.'

'How? My lord.'

He smiled. 'Under my command I have nearly a hundred servientes. I want you to lead eighty – ninety of them – and any others you choose – in a roundabout way. Head south. Cross the Kenet and keep going. Skirt it in a wide circle. Come at Louse Hille from behind.'

Warrene frowned. 'The servientes are not great warriors. They are as prone to fears of the mind as –'

Wintour grinned. 'I did not say they will fight. Burn the woods before you. Hack it down. Burn the ground before you. They will be driven on.'

The knight nodded slowly. 'And if they come at us? Or flee in another direction?'

He shook his head. 'They will not. We stand in their way. Reports say they are heading for the King's castle at Windesores. They cannot sneak past – we would just ride them down. They have trapped themselves in the woods. We will turn that to our advantage.'

Warrene nodded. 'Do I gather the men now – we can be –'

'No. Leave in the morning. We will have a scene – a falling out. You will take the troop elsewhere. After that is done, I will close the castle down, ensuring some of Alfred's men are out. The rebels will think we had a falling out.'

Warrene grinned. 'And we will drive them onto your lances.'

He nodded. 'Now go. Gather your men. Tell them the plan then take some rest. Tomorrow we begin to close in on the rebels.'

The knight saluted and withdrew. Wintour sent one of his soldiers to fetch the woman from his chamber. He met her outside Alfred's chamber. She was not as fresh as she could be, in body or years, but she wasn't unpleasing to the eye.

'My lord?'

Wintour smiled. She'd been a good lay. 'I recommended you to Alfred. He is in need of some – pleasure.' He drew her into his embrace and kissed her. She responded eagerly but he pushed her away. 'I think you and he will be together a long time.'

He opened the door and guided her in.

'My lord? Oh. Where are you? Are you –' her voice broke as she rounded the bed and dropped to her knees. 'Oh, sweet Mary –'

Wintour pulled her head back and drew the knife across her swanlike neck. Life bubbled out of her as she pitched forward over the constable's corpse.

Wintour stepped back, cleaning his knife, and stationed two of his men in front of the constable's chamber, with orders to tell anyone who asked that the constable was entertaining.

He returned to his chamber and poured himself some of the wine he'd commandeered from the constable's stores. It wasn't as good as what was served at court, but it came without side orders of cruelty and needless brutality.

"Dear sister," he wrote, settling down with parchment and quill, "this night I discovered treason and madness in the constable of Redinge. I am here at the King's bidding in what I believe an unrelated matter. I had wished to visit with you, but when my business is concluded here, as surely it will be in a matter of days, I go thence to Shrewsbury. Rufus honours me greatly. I hope you continue to remember your good fortune in the sanctuary of the nunnery, safe from the tides and the ripples of life's fortunes. Your brother in Christ, Wintour."

He marked the heavy parchment with his seal. It had been thought a foolishness of his father to teach both him and his sister how to write, but it saved the use of scribes, who could easily sell what they learnt from private confidences.

Not that I dare state plainly my private feelings for Rufus in letter or deed. That way lies the torture chamber.

He summoned a servientes and sent the runner off with the letter, commanding him to cross the Tames at Redinge.

Wintour leaned back in his chair. The fire was dying and the castle was silent. Looking at the hour candle he saw it was well past Lauds; almost dawn.

He stifled a yawn. It was too late to sleep. He'd have his public falling out with Warrene in a few hours. Not long after that he'd discover someone had murdered the constable and his wench and lock the castle down while he dealt with the rebels.

Once they're dealt with, I'm to Shrewsbury. They say de Belleme set a rat to gnaw the vitals of a knight who failed him. He shuddered. I'd rather Rufus, but only just. I'd rather be settled.

A small castle, he thought, bigger than this midden heap. A dutiful wife to bear my offspring. Mistresses to sate my need. Under tenants to fulfil my duty to the Crown. He closed his eyes. A red haired Saxon wench to warm my bed. Children – three sons and a daughter. He grinned. And bastards by the handful. Enough to give loyalty and trust. Safe from Kings and earls and border wars and traitorous servants –

A hammering at the door disturbed his musing. 'Who is it?'

'Warrene, my lord. You'd best come.'

He stomped over to the door and pulled it open. 'What is it?'

The knight looked grim faced. 'The rebels are come.'

He snorted. 'A ragbag of ruffians and outlaws attack a castle?'

Warrene nodded curtly. 'You'd best see for yourself. It's best viewed from the battlements of the north tower.'

There was light enough to see by but only just. The torches he'd commanded were mostly unlit.

'I gave the order –'

Warrene nodded. 'About an hour ago they began failing. I sent men to relight them. Some relit. Some men didn't return. I sent them out with archers, even with knights.'

He peered into the growing half-light. 'And?'

'BeauFyrd is dead. His throat was cut.'

Wintour turned to stare at Warrene. 'BeauFyrd was an old warrior, but no fool. He would have taken no chances, even with peasants.'

Warrene nodded sourly. 'A peasant with a pitchfork is still capable of killing a knight.'

'But not slitting their throat. How?'

The knight shook his head. 'I do not know. BeauFyrd commanded the servientes to light the torch. The man knelt to do so. He swears he heard and saw nothing. He lit it and stood up. BeauFyrd sat in the saddle, blood seeping onto his breastplate.'

Wintour shuddered. 'Stand aside from the battlements.'

He stepped closer to the edge. Within the failing torch light his men waited, mostly awake, on edge. Here and there a body lay, no more to rise.

Beyond the plateau, on the slope between the castle and Louse Hille stood a horde beyond expectation. There was something primeval about them.

He'd fought against ancient tribes of Saxons who wore nothing more than body paint. They had been fearless, terrifying opponents. But these men were stranger.

They wore woollen skirts, in shades of drab and dirty. They carried nothing more advanced than clubs or tree branches. They were uniformly filthy, ugly, and all the more terrifying because they stood in perfect silence.

'There must be five hundred of them.'

Wintour shook his head. 'If that is all –'

He looked to the south west: the Kenet, barely distinguishable at the best of times, was lost in the dimness. But between it and him –

Phalanx upon phalanx of leather clad warriors with long spears grounded. They wore polished silver helms and carried short swords at their belts. An officer walked behind them, his helmet adorned with a horse's tail of silver. Their skins were a burnished yellow nut brown.

Wintour crossed to the opposite battlement, staring in surprise. A squad of Janissaries stood between the castle and Redinge. He'd seen one once in Lundres, just like these, dressed in long white robes, their heads turbaned, wickedly sharp scimitars at their waists.

'Janissaries? What are Janissaries doing here? Why do they just watch?'

'I sent a scouting party to approach each.'

Wintour turned to look at the knight.

Warrene shook his head. 'Out of our sight must watch bowmen. None got anywhere near the troops. They have us penned in.'

To the south, blocking access to the swampy, low lying land, though he had no wish to head in that direction, stood an equally strange collection of warriors. They wore silk, and carried curved swords. They were a short race, their faces full of colour as if caught by the sun, their eyes – Wintour shuddered. Their eyes were like cats, or foxes, slanted and hooded.

'Form the warriors into blocks. Hold the knights in readiness, separate. We will use them to break one of these pinions. Then they can swoop round behind.'

Warrene nodded and departed. Moments later his men and the constable's were forming up, forming blocks to face the warrior host that surrounded them.

As the light rose he continued studying them, hoping to find a plan, hoping to detect a weakness, knowing he should be with his troops, not above, separate, but it was engrossing.

To the north stood the second largest assemblage of warriors.

'Where have they come from?'

There were pale brown skinned men, dressed in strange clothing akin to animal skins, all mottled greens and browns, but new: not the oft patched clothing of outlaws.

Beside them stood tall, bare chested warriors. Danes, surely, with their blond or silver hair. All were heavily muscled and carried large axes on their backs where the short, swarthy warriors seemed to carry nothing more than large knives.

Behind them stood the motley collection of outlaws and treacherous verderers. There was more than expected, and he realised half of them were neither, for the woodsmen carried bows and the others carried slings and wore pouches of stones at their waists.

In front of the Danes and the brown skinned knife men, stood three tall women.

Wintour whistled. They were as black as night. They wore more armour than he'd seen on all the others combined, and knife and sword hilts emerged from back, boots, waist, protruded from gloves and were taped to thighs.

Behind the horde, and scattered from west to south to east, were lines of Welsh bowmen. The whole host waited in silence.

Silently, without realising it, Wintour began to pray.

A figure detached from the assembled outlaws and strode towards the plateau. He appeared, curiously, to be unarmed. A herald, he thought mutely. What else would they have but a herald to announce them.

'My name is –' the wind snatched the man's words away. He knew he should descend, face the man, learn the message, but he was frozen to the spot, trapped.

'I have come to take –' the wind stole all sound, rising, pulling at him, and then it dropped and he heard another sound.

The primitive horde were stamping their feet. Left. Right. Left. Right. Left. Right. The sound was rising, amplifying, carried on the wind and the dust that was rising.

The phalanx of warriors raised their pikes. Thumped them down. Lifted. Dropped. Lifted. Dropped.

An eerie, high pitched sound shrieked along his nerve endings. The three black women had tilted their heads back and were producing the sounds of hell incarnate.

From the outlaws and the verderers and the slingers he could hear a low, slow, chant. He couldn't make out the words but some coldly rational part of his mind told him it was a complex four syllabled chant, not a simple war cry.

The chant swelled in volume and Wintour shuddered.

'JACK.'

The primitive horde had joined the chant, their voices crude and guttural but powerful in comparison to the outlaws.

A knight bolted from the plateau, lance couched, aiming for the horde. If they scatter and break, he thought, we may have a chance.

'A.'

He heard the whistling of arrows even over the chant. The knight's horse tumbled, throwing him towards the primitives, helpless. Still chanting in their slow way, two of the horde stepped forwards. As their clubs descended, as he heard the protesting shriek of metal denting, he bolted for the stairs.

'RUN.'

Wintour charged out of the gateway, sword in hand. The air was full of dust and the aftermath of whistling arrows. The screams and death cries of his men. The neighing of horses in pain. The smell of blood and piss and death. Warrene stared up at him, an arrow in his visor. One of the constable's men whimpered, an arrow pinning his wrist to the ground. Alicia in her nunnery. Mad, stammering King Rufus. The peasant wench he'd rolled and then killed. The thud of a hundred, a thousand, he knew not how many, feet against hard ground. The bowel-loosening ululations of the black skinned succubi. Other voices raised in song, in hymn, in chant, beautiful and ethereal and damning. His helm was still in his chamber. He had no shield. If they fire again –

'ARM.'

Through the dust and the haze and the sweat he could see the Janissaries closing in, silent as death. The phalanx of pikemen were advancing in step, their voices sweetly raised in battle hymn.

He backed away, nearly tripping over a weakly kicking horse. Still singing the Amazonian devils led the host towards what was left of his command. Stones filled the air. Arrows whistled by overhead.

He was untouched. Sacred. Protected.

'GED.'

The screams intensified behind him. The clash of steel. His hand was sweaty on the sword hilt. I've not been shriven. If this is the King's work: these are demons before me. He stooped and snatched a dagger from a fallen servientes.

One of the demon women was before him. Her eyes burned white as she gauged him, a sword in either hand. A knifeman flanked her on one side, a Dane on the other.

For Rufus he thought, striking, parrying her blow but just barely. The conflict burst around him and he was within the maelstrom. She was good. Parry. Parry. Strike. Pull back. The dance, the circle of steel, her swords were extensions of her arms and she had the reach of him.

'A.'

The sound roared all around him and he realised beyond the shrieking and the singing there were two chants, intertwining. The horde, he knew without looking, had not engaged. They had no need to. His men were being massacred. The horde simply chanted, slamming large palms to the ground where they squatted.

Steel on steel. No longer aware of the coolness where piss had dried on his thigh. Sweat in his eyes, blinking it away. The tiredness of his arms. The clash of steel – he'd somehow found another sword and fought the hell bitch with two swords, but he knew he couldn't last. His left hand was weaker; wouldn't hold. His muscles screamed in protestation.

'RAN.'

He could see the man, the grey haired herald, approaching behind the Amazon. He walked calmly, carrying no weapon. There was a great sadness on his face.

'DA.'

He swayed, fell forwards but retained his balance. Found he was on his knees.

Wintour looked up. The succubus had retreated, cleaning the single sword she carried.

'Personally,' the man said, 'I am very sorry it has come to this. But time is wrong. Reality is folding in upon itself.'

He sank to one knee beside him. Placed a supporting hand on his back. 'You have fought very well, but it will be forgotten. It will never have happened. Do you know Guy was persecuted for being a Cathar when that should not have happened for a hundred and fifty years? Time – no, history,' he stressed, 'is being compressed as alternate realities impinge on

218

this one. There can only be one present, and so all the extra energy – matter – goes into the past or future.'

The herald was an old man. He had a peasant face.

'The pain will soon be over. Tell me your name, sir Norman knight.'

'Win.' There was an emptiness growing inside him. A calmness. Rufus could terrify him no more. 'Tour. Wintour,' he managed, through cold lips slick with liquid.

'Well, Wintour. For a long time we have climbed a low slope. But we have passed the peak and are accelerating. Do you know what we are approaching?' He touched his arm gently. 'You cannot. We are approaching the big bang. Again. I suspect there have been countless others. A point will come when all this ceases to be. We cannot slow or stop it, and so we rush towards it. If we can time it right –'

There was a twinkle in the man's eye. The twinkle of Heaven or starlight. It had been so long since he'd gazed at the stars.

'– and time is everything, we will ride the wave. But,' he chuckled, 'in the mean while we rush towards Armageddon. We cannot hold back the night and so we rush towards it, to bring it about, that it is in a place and a manner of our choosing, that some of us might survive it to see a new solar system born.'

'W –' his lips felt thick. He didn't remember anyone giving him a drink, but his mouth, his throat, felt full. 'We?'

The chanting had finished. The wind had dropped. A woman appeared beside the old man, a woman with red hair. She wiped his mouth with a cloth. From her colouring he guessed her Saxon. Saw the bow slung over her shoulder. Welsh.

'We,' the man repeated. 'My name is Déraciné. This is Merián. I am sorry, Wintour. You are dying. After you are dead your bravery will be forgotten. The world, the universe, all the realities, will be sublimated. Forged anew. The Big Bang that brings about all creation.'

Behind the coldness there was a great warmth. He felt as if, chain by chain, he was being released from a heavy burden.

The woman – Merián – leaned in and kissed his cheek. Her kiss was a blossom of warmth on the coldness of his body. Once through the cold, once beyond the wall, it would be warm. The warmth of Heaven.

'That was for Armageddon,' she whispered. 'And Branwen. And Guy.'

He had forgotten he had hands until Déraciné took his hand.

'There will be a moment of pain, and then there will be Heaven,' the man whispered.

'Why? Why here?' he managed. He wanted to know more, but it was all he could ask.

There was metal beneath his fingers. The hilt of an unfamiliar sword.

'Because in Reading is a shop, a portal, a doorway. I was caught unawares, flung through it. I had been foolish. Made a stupid error. Doubted an innocent woman. Now I return with an army, an empire, for her. It is all I can give her.'

He felt the warmth of hands closing over his. Both the herald and the woman held his hand and braced his shoulders.

'This should not be,' said the man, 'we are trying to make it better.'

'We will remember you,' the woman said, 'in a new world.' She smiled, her grip tightening on his, and leant in and kissed him. 'Armageddon.'

She smelt of war, fire and blood and fear but behind all that the dank, terrifying smell of ancient woodlands, of deep places, of forgotten places.

'If you see my wife, my children,' the man sighed. Shook his head. 'They are gone. They may be in the future. But for now.'

Everything was unto the clouds. From a great distance. Something, some part of him, was hurtling downwards, but he was feeling safe and warm and comfortable and loved and he could see shapes approaching, people he knew, had known, had loved and lost.

'For Jacaranda,' said the voice of God, and all chains linking him to life fell away.

Jacaranda's Folly

The air was pregnant. Swollen. About to burst.

Jacaranda wrinkled her nose. There was a heavy tang that raised the hairs on her arms, on the back of her neck. She'd never smelt anything so heavy, so metal tasting, and yet like ash in her mouth.

She stepped away from the doorway. Something crunched underfoot and she drew her foot back. Bones, animal bones, picked clean and gleaming white lay in fragments.

The sky was a soaring blue overhead, a vast panoply of shades, tones and hues. A sun burned somewhere, hidden behind the high, derelict, oppressive buildings, but there was no warmth to the day. She tugged the jacket closed.

She was standing on a roadway of sorts, long since broken and cracked. Weeds grew up through the lumpy concrete, pale grey and purple tinged. Nothing else seemed alive. Jacaranda stretched her hand out to touch them, then jerked her fingers back at the electric charge.

The weeds seemed to turn to face her, then bent over, collapsing to ashen fragments. The ash lay in a heap, undisturbed in the still city.

There was a wall opposite her, the flanking wall of a building consumed by ivy. The ivy grew purple-black, coiling through the empty eyes of broken windows. The bricks were crumbling in places, turning to sand, eroded by time and whatever plagued the city.

Jacaranda looked up and down the street. Upwards was a broad roadway, similarly abandoned buildings under slow attack from vegetation and weeds, set back from the track.

Downwards from her the roadway was narrower, falling away to a bridge before rising again.

Something screamed and she jerked her head up, taking an involuntary step backwards. A scrawny bird beat its way across the panopoleptic sky, battling unseen elements.

'At least something still lives.'

The sound of her voice fell oddly; almost startled her. She turned around slowly. The town – city – whatever it was – was dead and yet still alive. Kept alive, she wondered, by the electricity that stained the air.

She strode over to the wall and the wall-creeper. Prepared for a shock, she grasped it with both hands and pulled.

Jacaranda flew across the roadway, her teeth buzzing, her fingers burning. She landed against the derelict façade of a building and closed her eyes.

Light burned in lines. Sparked. Fizzed.

The light became the veins in her eyelids. She opened her eyes.

The wall-creeper was dying without a sound, without a breath of wind to scatter its ashes. The eyes of the building stared blankly, blindly. Bricks crumbled. The fall of dust increased. The ivy withered and collapsed. Something crashed inside the building. Jacaranda put her hands down and winced.

Her palms, her fingertips, wherever she'd touched the ivy, were dark and bruised like blood blisters. She stood up slowly.

The building opposite was breathing clouds of dust into the air. The wall was half-collapsed: dust and decay withering in the daylight.

Jacaranda made her way down the roadway. Just a few paces down another bisected it, leading up to the right and straight, level, to the left.

She crossed to the middle of the junction and paused. Ancient, crumbling, ivy-entrapped buildings formed each corner and ran parallel to each roadway, with the exception of the building she had half destroyed.

Nothing moved. The town was still and quiet. Jacaranda closed her eyes.

Her hands twinged. She could smell the electricity in the air. There was almost no smell to the weeds or the ivy. No sound of water from the river below the bridge. The road beyond the bridge led up, up, up to the hill overlooking the town.

Jacaranda opened her eyes. 'Geographically the same.' She shuddered. Another Reading but a derelict, abandoned Reading. She headed down to the bridge.

No water flowed beneath it but an off-green sludge filled the banks, the colour of stagnant water. She sniffed. If there was any smell to it, it was buried in the ozone.

She bent down for a stone and tossed it over the bridge.

'Not quite Pooh-sticks, but –'

The stone was swallowed silently by the sludge. She shuddered and headed down from the bridge, then uphill.

By the time she reached the crown of the hill she was out of breath. Sweat trickled down her cheeks as she stopped, looking around.

A row of domestic buildings had succumbed to the ivy, crumbling in upon themselves, broken middle-fingered chimneys raised at the unnaturally blue sky.

The roadway split, the plateau stretching to the left. More of a jungle existed there, buildings consumed, broken down and regurgitated by the wall-creepers. Straight ahead the roadway descended from the plateau to south Reading –

– and there, in the distance, was something different. Something unexpected.

The roadway bent and curved, winding along the edge of the mostly domestic residences, heading for where the motorway led to other towns, other cities, in her world.

Beyond the town was an arid landscape. Gone were the trees and the wind turbines and village greens of her world, and the ivy-entrapped buildings of this world. Raw, glittering, bare rock fenced the far end of the town.

She could just see, at a distance of two or three miles, the roadway leading up. Except it just stopped. There was no motorway junction, only the glittering rocks.

And a silver-black tower, impossibly tall, like a lighthouse, watching over the derelict town.

Jacaranda headed towards it. There was nothing new to be seen. Whatever had killed the town, emptied it of inhabitants, had reached the outskirts. The smell of ozone was less oppressive, but away from the built-up heart of the town, still no wind blew.

The day turned hot. She removed the leather jacket. Her T clung to her. Sweat ran down her legs. Made her socks almost squelch. Away from the centre of the town it was hotter, more humid.

At last the roadway led up to the plateau and the strange tower. The roadway ended jaggedly, as if torn apart. The plateau was wider than she'd imagined or realised and solid: the landscape no longer mirrored her home town.

Resting central in the plateau was the immense, beacon-like tower. It had mirrors of burnished black and silver plate. It stood on four immense legs, each ending in a wheel whose circumference was far greater than her height. The ground was free of ruts: despite appearing to be mobile, it had not obviously moved recently. A ladder led up one leg, disappearing into the underneath of the tower.

Jacaranda walked around it slowly, paying equal attention to the landscape. It was as if a line had been drawn, beyond which the Reading she knew no longer existed. Beyond the line the terrain was multi-toned brown-gold, flecked with silver – minerals, she wondered.

The tower was the same on all sides. Blank-faced, black and silver, with only the single ladder for admission. It was so high she couldn't see the apex.

Jacaranda put her jacket on and began climbing the ladder. The metal was cold to the touch and odourless. She paused, wrinkling her nose. The air was fresher: it no longer smelt of ozone. No wind blew beneath the tower: it was cold.

The ladder stopped at a hatchway. She hesitated, then spun the wheel on the hatch. She felt it give, and pulled the hatch open.

A lighted room awaited her, with the faint sounds of electrical activity. She pulled herself up and over the lip, rolling away from the open hatch.

The room was reasonably lit, but dim in comparison to the sunlight below. It was square, utilitarian and small. Two open doorways led on, one to another room, one to a flight of stairs.

Jacaranda leaned over the hatch, pulled it up and sealed it. The other room was even smaller. Three walls were filled, floor to ceiling, with banks of machines. Colours flashed and the machines beeped, but no alarm seemed to have been given. The room was almost soporific.

She paused. She was hot and tired. It would be so easy just to rest, just to close her eyes for five minutes –

She pinched her palm, swearing as the pain from the burns flared again. I didn't come this far just to sleep. I could do that at home. She went through the doorway and up the stairs.

--

She was standing on the river of sludge. She wasn't sinking but she knew if she tried to move, she would. Both banks were out of reach.

She wrinkled her nose. There was a smell, but it wasn't of decay or stagnation. It wasn't ozone, either.

She was standing in a field. There was a doorway she had to go through, but ivy swarmed over the pillars. While she didn't move, the ivy remained inert. She knew if she moved, the ivy would consume the doorway: would eat her way home.

It was a clinical smell. The smell of hospitals or laboratories.

She remembered laboratories. Test tubes had been her toys. Bunsen burners her enemies in the battleground of her childhood. Periodic tables of a hundred different realities burned in her retinas. Matrices of time and causal effects on reality. Action to consequence sequences, chains interwoven with chaos and entropy. The DNA of fate and the randomness of humanity combined through reverse genetic engineering to create –

Jacaranda woke up screaming.

She was trapped. In a machine. A sterile room. White.

Her jacket hung on the back of a chair. Her clothes were neatly folded on the chair, clean, freshly washed.

She was wearing a medical gown. She was lying on a mattress within the machine, which extended over her feet. Hoops of white technological metal covered her hips and chest. Neither her hands nor feet were bound or chained in any way –

She looked at her hands, remembering the stinging pain. Her palms and finger tips felt soft, but otherwise unscarred by the electrical charge they'd received.

'You will find they are quite healed. I took the opportunity to repair several minor conditions you had.'

Jacaranda looked up. A silver haired man sat by the door. There was something vaguely familiar about his face, but the recognition slipped as quickly as it had appeared.

'Where am I?'

He chuckled.

'You are safe, healthy and well. You are in my house. My name is Gryffyn.'

He pressed a button on the arm of the chair and the white metal hoops slid back into the machine. He stood up smoothly.

'I will wait for you outside. Dress; when you are ready, join me and I will explain what I can.'

He let himself out and Jacaranda sat up.

She shivered. I feel – newborn. Soft. She ran her hand up her arm. The tattoo was still there. I don't know what I was imagining. She let the sleeve fall back. Examined her fingernails. I tore one yesterday. Middle finger, left hand.

The tear was still obvious, but no longer fresh. A couple of days, maybe. She pulled the chair over and began dressing.

What happened to me? I remember going into the room in the tower, then – Jacaranda frowned. I know I dreamed, but I can't remember them. Only a sense of – she shivered again. Being stuck, or caught somewhere.

Dressed, she stood up slowly. She felt stronger, fitter, than she'd expected to.

The door opened easily and she found herself in a small office. The man – Griffin – sat in one of the chairs at a table. The room smelt of proper coffee, filtered coffee, and fresh-baked biscuits.

Gryffyn indicated the other chair. A freshly poured cup of coffee steamed before it; three biscuits on a silver platter beside it.

'Help yourself. I always take coffee about this time.'

Jacaranda sat down slowly. 'Where, exactly, am I?'

Gryffyn smiled. He had the ghost of a beard, softening his lean face. Was dressed like a businessman. 'This is not your world. You emerged from the heart of destruction. Came through the demarcation zone.'

Jacaranda frowned. 'I don't –'

Gryffyn laughed. 'The portal. You come from a different version of this reality. How is it different?'

She shook her head, lacing her fingers around the cup. 'What destroyed the town?'

His laugh died away. He scowled. 'The portal. The doorway. The heart of destruction. Call it what you will. It is a fracture, and like all fractures, it is gradually growing.'

She took a sip of the coffee. It smelt wonderful, but the taste didn't quite match the aroma.

'I own the bookshop. I've known about the doorway – for a while.' She pulled a face. 'Certainly nowhere near as long as Henghist knew.' She looked up at Griffin. 'Can you tell me,' she began, but stopped at the intensity of his stare.

'You're Jacaranda?' He smacked his hand to his forehead, and got to his feet. 'Oh, my dear, I am so sorry, come, there is no time.'

She put the cup down as he touched her elbow. 'What's the hurry?'

Gryffyn sighed heavily. 'It's my fault.' Seeing her look he shook his head. 'We need to go. I'll explain on the way.'

She stood up, grabbing one of the biscuits.

'Follow me,' he said, running for a door she'd not noticed before.

It opened onto a stairwell and he began jogging down.

'How did you recognise me? What's the rush?'

Gryffyn glanced back at her, not slowing his pace. 'There is a standing order from the Council of Judges. Anyone that comes through the demarcation zone is to be arrested. When you were in the medi-machine I sent a message. There'll be a squad of guards on the way to arrest you.'

They came to a landing and he was through the door in an instant. Spiral stairs led down steeply.

'If you know I'm alien –'

He looked up at her and his face was suddenly familiar. 'If you're Jacaranda then you're my daughter-in-law.'

Jacaranda stared. Stumbled. He caught; balanced her.

'We need to hurry. You need to hurry.'

The stairs ended and she found herself in a familiar room.

'I climbed up here. This is the tower.'

Gryffyn glanced up from where he was undoing the hatch and nodded. 'We keep watch on the demarcation zone. It will destroy the world eventually.'

She nodded, recollection returning. 'While I was in that machine –'

'The medi-machine.'

Jacaranda nodded again. 'I dreamt. I'd forgotten, earlier. But –'

Gryffyn nodded hastily, releasing the hatch. 'The medi-machine does an excellent job of healing superficial problems – like your hands – but it has a tendency to cause dreams in users. They are,' he shrugged. 'The dreams of a machine? No one quite knows. But they are harmless.'

He ran to the other room, the machine room, and returned with a backpack. 'Come on, Jacaranda. We must – you must – get out of here quickly.'

He was through the hatch and was descending even as he spoke. Jacaranda followed him rapidly.

It was mid-morning. The plateau seemed unchanged, though the ground near the wheels appeared flattened.

Gryffyn was looking round in concern. 'The guards aren't here yet, but they'll be here soon. You must go.'

Jacaranda looked at Griffin, her father-in-law, and hesitated. 'I never had a chance – Henghist never spoke of you. I didn't know –'

He waved away her concerns. 'I wish we had more time, daughter, but we do not.'

She looked out at the surrounding arid lands. 'There's no sign of anyone on the way –'

Gryffyn snorted. 'They'll come in air-cars. Here, take this backpack. Open it when you get to your world.' He smiled warmly, a little sadly.

Jacaranda glanced again at the arid land. 'Did the – portal – do that?'

He shook his head. 'We destroyed our own lands to seal in the demarcation zone. None enter the arid lands except watchers – like myself – and guards.' He passed over the backpack. 'But go. Hurry. The guards will cross into the edge of the demarcation zone if they have to.'

She slung the rucksack on her back. 'Thank you. I wish – I would have liked –'

Gryffyn nodded. 'I would have liked to spend more time with my daughter. I wish I could have showed you my world, damaged though it has become.' He sighed, but smiled. 'I wish I could have told you about Henghist and Horsa. When they were children. That is a side of them you will not get to find out about. But go, please. I don't want the guards to catch you.'

She nodded slowly. Griffin closed the distance between them and she bowed her head; he kissed her forehead.

'Go, child. Safely reach your world. Look after my sons.'

Jacaranda hesitated. I should tell him about Horsa. About Bridget. But I cannot break his heart. I can always return, with more care, later. She leaned down, kissed his cheek, and turned away.

She jogged downhill, expecting to hear the sounds of pursuit at any time. The backpack was heavy but she felt refreshed. Increased her pace to a run. The roadway back to the plateau above the town was long, open, exposed. They might come as far as the plateau. Once I'm descending from there I should be safe.

Finally, she was rising to the plateau. She paused, though not in need of a breather, and looked back. The tower was just visible, but there was something else, something mobile –

Jacaranda resumed running.

In no time at all she was crossing the bridge and rising, rising towards the portal and the way back to her shop.

She crossed the junction. The ivy-denuded building had not collapsed any further. She spared it a glance as she placed her hand on the door. Pushed it open –

– And then she was in her shop lobby. She wiped her brow, remembering the backpack and removing it.

'They destroyed part of their own world for fear of the portal.' She shook her head, unclasping the ties on the rucksack. 'Why do they fear it so much?'

She loosened the drawstring on the backpack and pulled it open. 'What did Griffin mean I won't get the chance –'

The slow, muffled beeping penetrated her consciousness and she looked down.

There was a clock. Figures, counting down.

Zero-five. Zero-four. Zero-three.

Jacaranda pulled the door open, Zero-two, feeling the slight resistance as it opened into a different reality, and grasped the rucksack and flung it, Zero-one, bomb and all, out.

Zero –

She shut the door.

– zero.

Cornix Sinistra

'I was there, at the beginning of the end. I was only a young man then, and she,' he wheezed, feeling the breath rattle in his chest, 'she was different. She was time incarnate. She was alien. She was –' he breathed noisily again, closing his eyes.

"She was old, older, but not old. She moved with the sleekness of a wealthy person who lived in one of the cities, safe, beyond reach of the chronometer's devastating effects. She could have been one of the old order, but she was their antithesis, their destruction. She was no rebel though, no outcast urchin living in the Plains of Time."

He could still see her clearly, despite all that had happened in the meantime.

"Silver hair mostly, a little black, and tall. She came from the rocks at the edge of Sapphire Mountains. It was a place many of us called home, close to one of the lesser chronometers. There were plants and animals to survive on and we were free, dangerous, constantly exposed to the chronometer. Occasionally someone came from the city, wanting to experience time, but we let them be. They were ageless, near immortal. We lived and breathed –"

He broke off, coughing. She had warned him and he had chosen to stay with her. Chosen. I wouldn't change my decision.

"He stood up as she approached. She was wearing strange clothing, not the long, loose robes favoured by most in the arid land, but clothing that followed her shape. She was long legged: wore dark trousers and boots. She wore a red short sleeved shirt, surely an undershirt. It clung to her torso in a way he'd not seen before. Her eyes were blue and there was none of the haughtiness of the old guard in her expression but she was old but not angry and only the old guard, the rich and prosperous, lived in the cities, immune to the effects of the chronometers.

'You – you're –'

She smiled. 'I came from up in the mountains.'

His two companions looked up, staring. With curses they took off, scattering dust and stones in their flight.

'I'm Takahe. Who – what – are you?'

She frowned. 'I'm Jacaranda. I came from –'

The name was known to his listeners, the storyteller saw. They had come searching for her, after all, albeit separately. It was his idea to cloak and hood them: the dust on the plains was terrible, and they'd accepted his suggestion.

'Lady, you're time. It's like –' he glanced down the trail where his comrades had fled. 'It's an itch. I can feel it in my skin, my bones, all the way down to my cells. You're aging me.'

She shook her head, transferring the bag she carried from one shoulder to the other. 'I'm,' she paused, sighing, shaking her head. 'Is it always this warm?'

Takahe looked up. The sun loomed high in the sky. In the plains and mountains it seemed to flow, never settling, never permanent. One of the city dwellers had tried pulling his leg, telling him in the city the sun remained constant, unmoving, but he knew that was a lie. City dwellers thought the urchins were gullible, forced as they were to dwell in the places where time held sway.

He shrugged. He wore nothing more than a rag, his skin toned by life in the constant sun, his eyes permanently narrowed. 'We live in the light. The light affects us all, unlike time, which was banished from the cities –' he broke off. He'd learnt the words by rote, every child did, but no child had ever come across a woman like this before. She was time, but beautiful, even as she aged him.

'I would like to see one of your cities. Could you point me towards it?'

Takahe hesitated. I could send her to the nearest city but they wouldn't admit her, unless they'd become time-blind. I can feel what she's doing to me. She's stronger than the lesser chronometer. He grinned evilly. She could shake the city up. It might be dangerous but it could be fun. 'I'll take you there.'

She frowned. 'Didn't you say – I aged you? It would be dangerous. And if you live in the mountains, are you welcome in the city?'

He shrugged. 'I can get you into the city lady. I reckon they won't know what you are. I can show you it all.'

'Are you sure?' she asked, wiping her brow. Her face was flushed with warmth; sweat gathered on her arms.

'It'll be fun,' he added, smiling for an instant then looking away. Fun. I sound like a child.

'Listen,' she said, stepping closer, 'you don't have to if it's dangerous. Cities can be scary places.'

Takahe sneered. 'Ha. The city will have more to fear. C'mon. It's this way.'

'Give me a moment,' she said, turning her back, removing the pack.

Takahe looked down to the plain. The city was out of sight. Out of sight, out of reach of time, as they said. He'd never been before, but it was easy to find. The land became more arid around the cities. Something to do with the inability of seeds to propagate without time. Creatures didn't like going near the cities either. Despite the warmth he shivered. She was alien. Intoxicating. Time. If the city discovered her true nature – but she'd appeared to him, not a city dweller boy.

'I'm ready.'

She was stuffing something white and flimsy into her pack, not looking up at him. The undershirt clung to her in a way it hadn't before. All the girls he knew either dressed like him, with a rag knotted around their hips, or wore loose robes. Her undershirt clung to her breasts. He felt an intoxicating thrill. He could see the impression of her nipples against the material –"

'Get on with the tale. We don't need to know all your dirty thoughts.'

The storyteller nodded, coughing, wheezing. 'Forgive an old man his foolishness. I am older now than she was then, though I was younger then.'

"Takahe led the stranger down the mountain. If he hadn't been used to the mountain ways he might have been hard pressed to keep up with her. Her long legs ate up the distance but he had no fear where she showed caution.

At last they reached the mountain's edge, the start of the plain. The sun had wobbled but now remained in place. He was tired though he wouldn't admit it. They stopped. She was bent over, hands on her knees. He could see her undershirt was sopping wet. Sweat dripped off her face.

'Is there any shade? Anywhere we can sleep, out of the sun?'

Takahe shook his head. 'It's cooler in the mountains. That's another reason we're outcast – we like the shade and the height. They say we're not true city dwellers.'

She looked up at him. 'I'm tired. I need to sleep. It's too hot.'

'Takahe –" he looked up at the three listeners to his tale.

The hooded robes they wore kept their faces in deeper shadow than the shallow cave they all sat in. If they only knew – when they knew –

"Takahe fashioned shade for her and she slept awhile."

He sat cross legged. She removed her undershirt, which was sodden, and curled up around him with her head in his lap so that he could lean on her shoulders, sheltering her from the sun.

"When she woke up Takahe led her off to the city. It was a walk of many hours and many rests."

At the third stop, and at each subsequent stop, she removed her boots and trousers, and curled up, her head in his lap. She wore nothing but a cloth, and that not a rag, though perspiration had made it sodden.

He became used to the warmth and strength and softness of her body. There were rings around her eyes and her hair was matted and greasy when she walked, but while he dozed over her, sheltering her from the sun, he dreamed she was a Goddess. She stood before him in his dreams, with her alabaster skin turning soft pink and orange as the sun touched it, with her silver hair and blue eyes and her rosé tipped breasts bared for him and every time he woke up with an erection, but thankfully it passed by the time she woke. Nothing would have embarrassed him more than to have her wake up then.

'Are you just going to stare into the fire or are you going to tell us of this 'cursed alien'?'

The storyteller looked up. It was a different speaker; the first turned his head but didn't respond. He wondered why they pretended not to know Jacaranda.

"Takahe took her to the city but before they got close a party intercepted them. There were half a dozen guards, carrying their electric spears. Two young noble children, taken outside the city for the first time, barely able to walk, and a younger nobleman with blond hair and a youthful, arrogant expression.

'You're not welcome here woman. You, urchin, take one step closer and it'll be your last.'

She pulled Takahe back. 'I only wanted to see your city. This young man has done nothing wrong.'

The speaker scowled. 'He is a rebel. His family chose to live outside the city. They feel the effects of time. They are no longer welcome.'

She let go of him and took a step closer. 'I am a visitor to your land. I come in peace. I only wish —'

She broke off as the guards aimed their long spears at her, nozzles open.

'You are a carrier,' the speaker snapped, 'you age us just by your presence. No city will welcome you. Take one step closer and the guards will eliminate the threat you pose.'

'Is there nothing I can do to prove I mean you no harm?'

The speaker grinned, baring his teeth.

'It has been a number of the urchin kind's years since any have checked the Great Chronometer. That will be a worthy task for you – and your friend.'

Takahe sucked in a breath. The Great Chronometer. To see it, to perceive time itself – it was far out in the arid land – was to gather years in days. It could turn a babe to an old man in a week.

'Takahe? What's wrong?'

He looked up at the lady. He still thought of her as a lady. Her name was strange, alien, angelic. She was beautiful and he was growing in her presence and no one else could say they nestled an angel in their laps and yet – and yet. The Great Chronometer.

'Is it safe?'

He nodded slowly. 'I think, for you, it will be.'

She raised an eyebrow. 'And for you?'

Takahe shrugged. 'I said I would stay with you. I will.'

She leant over and embraced him; kissed his cheek.

'You will have to circumnavigate the city. We will not allow you in.'

The envoy was grinning smugly.

Takahe reached out and took her hand. 'It is this way."

The walk was long and interesting. She told him of her world, of how, from what he could understand, she owned a place selling parchment. A lot of it meant nothing to him. Living free of the cities they had a shorter life. A girl he'd known had gone from wearing only a rag to wearing a loose robe as her body changed. There had been a marriage not long after, and a birth, new life. There had even been the cessation of life that came to all, but faster in the hills and plains than the city.

She was getting stronger, no longer needing to rest so often. Once out of sight of the city she'd stripped off, all the way, then tied her undershirt round her hips. They walked side by side. Sometimes she held his hand. Sometimes she put her arm round his shoulders.

When they did rest, she would sit cross legged and he would straddle her thighs. Sitting like that he was almost taller than her. She would lay her head against his neck. He would fall asleep, no longer dreaming of her as an angel or Goddess, while she slept in his arms.

'Tell us of this great chronometer.'

The third speaker was a woman. He had brought the three, separately, to his cave where he waited for the end of the world. He was too old to care that the ground heaved and the skies cracked and wind blew across the plains and the sun was mobile, moving its position. She had brought destruction in her wake; brought the first sunset. He'd heard how that had killed many of the old guard. They just couldn't cope with change, and Jacaranda had remade the world.

"For time they walked. Days – had no meaning then. Hours only existed around the chronometers. It was the furthest he'd ever walked, and just before sleeping each time he wondered how long he would last, the closer he got to the Great

Chronometer. But he would not abandon Jacaranda. Whatever the cost.

Finally the arid nature of the land changed. The rock softened and weeds grew between boulders, and a brisk wind blew. The rocks gave way to grass, and here and there low, shrub-like trees blossomed. The wind eased the heat somewhat. His feet were hard; unfeeling. Jacaranda abandoned her boots and her feet were soft but gradually she became used to it.

In the distance, like a finger, something rose tall and dark and he headed them towards it. It became easier to find shade to rest in but she pushed on, as much for himself, he thought, as to get there.

Finally it came into sight and details could be seen."

In the cooler, time sensitive lands, he would lie in her arms. He had sheltered her from the sun. Now she sheltered him. He would lie with his head on her chest. He had seen her naked so often that her nudity no longer affected him. Now she was Jacaranda, a friend, a confidant, someone to whom partial or full nudity was nothing.

"Each face was about fifty metres long, and the Great Chronometer was five faced. It was made of steel, perfect, uncorroded, polished as brightly as silver but far stranger. Each side was made of parallel pipes running from out of the ground to a height of, he guessed, close to a hundred metres tall. It was monstrous in size. Higher up, beyond their sight so close were they, were actual clock faces.

'So this is the Great Chronometer,' whispered Jacaranda.

He reached out to touch it but she pulled him back. 'Let me. You're the time sensitive one, remember. Don't touch it.'

She set off around the faces. He retreated several steps and sat down to wait for her."

He found some white flowers and twined them into a necklace and crown for her. When she came back he offered them to her and she giggled like a younger woman, taking the crown and putting it on but bending her head so he could loop the necklace over, the white standing out against the cream of her skin, glowing warmly from the constant sun.

He bent his head and began kissing her small breasts and her hands were in his hair and she pulled him away and he wondered whether he'd gone too far and then she was kissing him, hard, on the mouth –

'Did she come back to him?' the woman asked.

The storyteller nodded, distracted for a moment. He could still smell the grass and the warmth of her body and the feel of her body moving against his and the distant sound of bird song which had echoed, initiated even, their own cries of pleasure.

'Yes. There was nothing to be seen and if she had done anything, she didn't tell him.'

"Jacaranda led him a distance away and then stopped. She retrieved something from her pack, and turned to face the Great Chronometer.

'Nobody will believe me if I don't.' She giggled. 'Not that I could tell anyone. But I'd like proof I'm not going mad.'

It was a small metallic object. She slid the top part up and aimed it at the Great Chronometer. He wondered what she was going to do.

There was a click, and he felt a great wrenching pain as if someone had ripped his innards out, and a loud bang, and Jacaranda was flung aside.

He rushed to her and her hand was blistered, her fingers burnt where she'd been holding the object, which was nowhere to be seen. He helped her to her feet, knowing she was wrong. He looked up at the chronometer. It was still there, unchanged and lifeless. He looked at Jacaranda.

She had always been time, but now she was Time. He could feel it in her arms, in every touch of her body."

'Every touch of her body? What are you intimating, storyteller?'

He looked up at the speaker. 'I know you are strangers to this land, seeking answers.' He shrugged. 'Proof. Our people are time sensitive. Long ago, when time existed freely, the scientists waged war against it. They contained it in chronometers scattered across the world. The Great, and an incalculable number of lesser. Out of sight of these they built cities where time had no purchase. A few people rebelled; they went to live in the plains and mountains that they might experience passing time. Occasionally a nobleman or woman would travel out of the city to gain experience. To gain, or lose, time. They lived long, unchanging, lives, free from disease, pollution, death.'

'Very interesting, but how does this relate to Jacaranda?'

He recognised the voice of the second speaker, the most vocal, the one to whom Jacaranda meant most.

'She came from another world. Time – was part of her. She aged Takahe just by being in his company. But after the incident at the Great Chronometer –'

'Tell us,' said the woman.

"They walked on, away, back towards the city. Takahe knew she was different. The aging effect she had on him was stronger. Time, the journey, seemed to pass quicker, until the city reappeared."

When they rested, which was infrequently, he would look at her mutely and she would gaze back. He wanted to touch her, to hold her, to be with her, but he knew that would age him rapidly. Despite the rising heat she dressed, no longer teasing him with the sight of what he'd once had.

"Two guards came out to meet them, much further out than the other party had.

'Go,' one snarled, raising his spear, finger on the trigger, 'get away from here.'

She stared, surprised and shocked. 'I checked on the Great Chronometer like I was told. I have —'

'Look behind you bitch,' the other snarled, 'you've brought time with you.'

Takahe turned also. Her steps were visible in the arid land. Each was an oasis of weeds, breaking through the stony ground. Further back a flower blossomed.

'Back away.' One of the guards stepped closer, spear levelled, finger on the trigger. 'Back away or so help me —'

'Jerik —' the other warned.

The nearer guard was black haired, except at the temples, which were silver. His hands shook as he glanced at his comrade.

'What?'

The silver was spreading.

'Oh my God,' whispered Jacaranda.

Jerik turned back to face her. 'What have you done to me?'

'I can help,' she said, taking a step forwards.

Takahe watched, frozen in horror, for once bereft of time to warn Jacaranda as the second guard raised his spear, depressing the button.

The electrical energy struck her full on, bending her arms and legs backwards, tossing her away in petrified silence.

Takahe rushed to where Jacaranda had been thrown. She lay in a bundle, limp, unmoving. He knelt down. Hesitated, then stretched his hand to feel for the pulse in her neck."

'What — what happened?'

'Is she —'

The storyteller shrugged. 'I am no scientist. Our greatest days are long past, the skills of the ancients forgotten. But that day,' he shook his head. 'Her name is cursed. She brought time back with her. For an arid land, we have had thunder a lot recently. The ground heaves. Flowers grow in stone. The sun sets and city dwellers think they have gone blind. The old order is in ruins, too slow to change. The youngsters,' he coughed, wheezing. His chest felt tight. 'They don't have the experience. It's primitive survival. We were two halves, the city dwellers and the time dwellers. Time had been unleashed and it rips, eddies, drowns, tears this world apart as it remakes it.'

'And Jacaranda did all that?' the woman asked.

The storyteller nodded. Afterwards, while she'd lain atop him, their passion spent, she'd told him of her family. Of Henghist, her husband, who had found the gateway when he was a child and come through it with his brother Horsa. How Henghist had lied to her all their marriage until events forced his hand. How he had wanted a child to continue what he'd started and she'd wanted his child but it hadn't happened.

Of Horsa, the brother, whom Henghist had cut off from the portal, though he'd not told her why. Horsa had committed suicide over it apparently.

And of Horsa's daughter Bridget, the daughter of two worlds, who'd disappeared not long after finishing studying.

He'd let the words wash over him at the time. He was thinking there would be a hundred such occasions, a thousand such.

'Where is she now? Where's her body? I want to see. I want proof.'

He managed to chuckle, though it turned into a cough. 'The world tears itself apart. Walls fall. Buildings collapse. The ground acts like the sea.' He shook his head. 'A single body in the plains? It is gone, long gone.'

'You bastard,' the man hissed, half standing but remembering the low height of the cave. 'She is my wife.'

The storyteller nodded. 'You are Henghist then.'

The man stared, his face just visible within the hood. 'How do you know me?'

'And you,' he continued, pointing at the woman, 'would be Bridget.'

The woman lowered her hood to reveal long, dark brown hair; a slightly chubby face but an intelligent gaze. 'I am Bridge now.'

There was only one the third could be. 'You are Déraciné?'

The second man lowered his hood to gasps of shock and surprise.

'I am Horsa.'

'Father.'

There was a look of pure hatred on the woman's face, stronger and purer than any the envoy or the guards had even given Jacaranda.

'Why did you do it?' she demanded. 'Why were you too cowardly to stand up for me?'

'You're supposed to be dead,' said Henghist icily.

The storyteller leaned back. He had retrieved Jacaranda's body. The destruction that had followed in her wake had been slow but inexorable. He had taken her to a secret place, a sacred place, and left her there. If the world survived she would be venerated. If it didn't – well, it would hardly matter then.

Light was dying. Sounds were fading away.

He saw her then, and didn't know if she was a Goddess of his people or a delirium brought on by imminent death.

She was fair skinned, with long black hair falling unbound to her hips. A dozen or more gold bracelets shone from each wrist. Her ears were ornamented with rings and studs and there was a silver stud in her nose. Her eyes were silver – all colours – in the painted shadows. Her hair was parted in the centre and gold jewellery adorned the parting, ending with a ruby at her forehead. A dozen necklaces, strung with beads of oak and gold and lapis lazuli and ebony fell between her heavy breasts.

She was a mother. She was a Goddess. She was death.

Takahe smiled, and knew he would die with a smile on his face. His spirit ran to her and he knew he was not forsaken for his part in the destruction of his world and she wrapped her arms around him and the cave was gone, and the world was gone, and he was gone.

Epilogue

The end is not the end.

As might be expected from a work of speculative apocalyptic fiction, the end remains to be told. The end is being told, out there, in the world, all around us. Or, more specifically, in 'Armageddon Angel'.

In 'Armageddon Angel' we will be led even further down the ever-darkening path towards Armageddon. The Big Bang. Apocalypse. Ragnarök. The Rapture. Call it what you will, it is coming.

There is a bookshop. There will be fire and pain and death. There will be technology and cruelty, love and lust, hope and hopelessness.

The Oracle will reveal more about the Armageddon Key. The dead will walk and not be dead. Bridge's mentor will return. Wizerbowski will choose sides in the upcoming extinguishment. Déraciné will lead his army to war to defend Jacaranda. Courtney will make his mark. Miles and Louise seek retribution from the Unforsaken Land, and out of Morocco, Amaranthaceae will return.

And Jacaranda, Bridge, Déraciné, and Wizerbowski must try to stop that which cannot be stopped.

About Steven C. Davis

Steven C. Davis is the author of 'The Bookshop between the Worlds' pair of alternate-Earth novels, 'The Lore of the Sælvatici', part of a folk-horror retelling of the Robin Hood mythos, and co-author, with S. J. Stewart, of 'The Heart's Cog' series of NSFW action-adventure novels.

They are the organiser of the 'Raising Steam' festivals and the 'Raising Steam' downloads – all in aid of their chosen charity, New Futures Nepal, of whom they are a trustee. The 'Raising Steam' downloads are a global phenomenon, gathering Steampunk and alternative independent and unsigned musical artists from the UK and around the globe.

They are the host of the Gothic Alternative Steampunk and Progressive (GASP) radio show which goes out every Thursday at 8pm (UK time). GASP plays music without borders and is deliberately eclectic, playing the best in unsigned and independent regardless of genre.

About Carolin Southern

Carolin is an artist and illustrator residing in the Scottish Highlands. She primarily works in traditional media, and her art encompasses horror, fantasy, Gothic themes, Pagan imagery and the occult. In her spare time, she plays eerie melodies on her harmonium, psalterie and collection of unusual wind instruments, enjoys hill-walking and wild-camping (the creepier the forest the better). She has a degree in Architectural Technology and is now studying History & Cultural Studies. Her primary love is historical architecture. Her Instagram accounts are @dragonandcatdesigns for her artwork and @architecturallygothic for her architectural photography.

GASP's Trading Card # 1
Valentine Wolfe

Bio: Two morbidly fascinated musicians combining ambient solo bass, brutal distortion, electronica, and 18th Century opera to tell a story of the macabre.
Link: valentinewolfe.bandcamp.com
Raising Steam: Appears on 'Raising Steam III'. Raisingsteam.bandcamp.com

Listen to the Gothic, Alternative, Steampunk and Progressive (**GASP**) Radio show every Thursday 8 – 11pm (UK time). Search for Steven C. Davis on mixcloud.com

Currently Available

'Cornix Sinistra'

'Steam Flashes'

'Tenebrosian Tales'

Forthcoming Releases
'Armageddon Angel'– 2021.

'Texts from the Shadows I' – 2021

'Lore of the Saelvatici' – 2021

'The Heart's Cog Imperative [parts 1, 2 and 3]' by Steven C. Davis
& S. J. Stewart – 2021

Limited editions available from here:
https://www.etsy.com/uk/shop/TenebrousTexts/

Find Steven's work on Amazon here:
https://smile.amazon.co.uk/Steven-C-Davis/e/B006TZ8MFA?ref=sr_ntt_srch_lnk_15&qid=160656974
6&sr=1-15

Hope you enjoy it!

all the best

Steven C Parr

Printed in Great Britain
by Amazon

59652450R00145